Letters

FROM Vinnie

For my parents, Peggy and John Stack,
my husband, Steve,
and our children, John, Brian, Bridget, and Kathleen
(my heart, too, is a crowded place)

Letters
FROM Vinnie

Maureen Stack Sappéy

FRONT STREET
Asheville, North Carolina
1999

Acknowledgments

My gratitude to the Civil War historians who offered their time and expertise, including the living historian Bill Blake and the former and current directors of the United States Civil War Center at Louisiana State University, David Madden and Leah Wood Jewett; my thanks, too, to the Music Division and the Special Collections Division of the Library of Congress. I am also grateful to my stepmother, Barbara, for her constant encouragement; my friend Regina Rheingrover, who served as an inspiration for my creation of Vinnie's friend Regina; my editor, Katya Rice, for her invaluable help in revealing the grace and strength in Vinnie's voice; and my publisher, Stephen Roxburgh, for his dedication to excellence and his faith in my belief that Vinnie's story was worth the telling.

Library of Congress Cataloging-in-Publication Data
Sappéy, Maureen Stack.
Letters from Vinnie / by Maureen Stack Sappéy.
p. cm.
Summary: A fictionalized account of the Washington, D.C., Civil War years experienced by Vinnie Ream the sculptress, best known for the statue of Abraham Lincoln that is in the Capitol building.
ISBN 1-886910-31-6 (alk. paper)
1. Ream, Vinnie, 1847-1914—Juvenile fiction.
2. Washington, D.C.—History—Civil War, 1861-1865—Juvenile fiction.
[1.Ream, Vinnie, 1847-1914—Fiction. 2.Washington, D.C.—Civil War, 1861-1865—Fiction.
3. United States—History—Civil War, 1861-1865—Fiction. 4. Sculptors—Fiction.
5. Lincoln, Abraham, 1809-1865—Fiction. 6. Letters—Fiction.] I.Title
PZ7.S2388Le 1999
[Fic]—dc21 98-52337

Letters
FROM Vinnie

Maureen Stack Sappéy

FRONT STREET
Asheville, North Carolina
1999

Acknowledgments

My gratitude to the Civil War historians who offered their time and expertise, including the living historian Bill Blake and the former and current directors of the United States Civil War Center at Louisiana State University, David Madden and Leah Wood Jewett; my thanks, too, to the Music Division and the Special Collections Division of the Library of Congress. I am also grateful to my stepmother, Barbara, for her constant encouragement; my friend Regina Rheingrover, who served as an inspiration for my creation of Vinnie's friend Regina; my editor, Katya Rice, for her invaluable help in revealing the grace and strength in Vinnie's voice; and my publisher, Stephen Roxburgh, for his dedication to excellence and his faith in my belief that Vinnie's story was worth the telling.

Library of Congress Cataloging-in-Publication Data
Sappéy, Maureen Stack.
Letters from Vinnie / by Maureen Stack Sappéy.
p. cm.
Summary: A fictionalized account of the Washington, D.C., Civil War years experienced by Vinnie Ream the sculptress, best known for the statue of Abraham Lincoln that is in the Capitol building.
ISBN 1-886910-31-6 (alk. paper)
1. Ream, Vinnie, 1847-1914—Juvenile fiction.
2. Washington, D.C.—History—Civil War, 1861-1865—Juvenile fiction.
[1.Ream, Vinnie, 1847-1914—Fiction. 2.Washington, D.C.—Civil War, 1861-1865—Fiction.
3. United States—History—Civil War, 1861-1865—Fiction. 4. Sculptors—Fiction.
5. Lincoln, Abraham, 1809-1865—Fiction. 6. Letters—Fiction.] I.Title
PZ7.S2388Le 1999
[Fic]—dc21   98-52337

CONTENTS

1861

1 8 6 1

My dear friend Regina,

Yesterday I envied birds their wings, for I longed to fly northeast to our Nation's capital city. There I would have alighted upon the dome of the Capitol building above the crowd gathered on the steps around our new President. Bowing my feathered head, I would have listened carefully as Mr. Lincoln spoke.

Sadly, I have no wings, and so I must practice patience until I can read about Mr. Lincoln's Inauguration. I do hope the newspapers here in Arkansas faithfully report every word of his Inaugural Address.

Last night, in celebration of our new President, Ma made a grand supper of pork stew and slices of sugared bread—rare treats for us these days. My family has known some days of hunger, but Spring is upon us and Ma has newly planted her garden.

After supper, my family gathered by the hearth, and Ma poured us glasses of cold cider. Wishing to reveal my respect for President Lincoln, I waited for a quiet moment and declared myself a Republican! My sister, Mary, laughed and said girls shouldn't concern themselves with politics since we cannot vote, but Pa admired my interest in Mr. Lincoln's new political party. He raised his glass and said, "As a family, we must heartily support our President."

Oh, Regina—I'm ashamed to admit what happened then! My brother, Bob, leapt up from his chair and stood glaring down at Pa. Bob looked almost giant, for he is much taller than other boys of fifteen years. Even his voice sounded giant, loud and angry, when he shouted "No!" at my pa. Bob called Mr. Lincoln an ugly baboon, and he screamed something that I didn't understand, about the secession of states.

As Bob stood there with his back to the hearth, the light of the fire encircled him; his red hair looked like bits of flame, and his blue eyes blazed as though his soul had ignited. His enraged face was the face of a fearsome stranger, not that of my beloved brother.

Poor Ma was affrighted and Pa demanded an apology, but Bob refused and stomped up the steps to his room.

My parents and Mary sat without speaking. Curiosity overcame my own silence, and I asked what Bob had meant by secession of states. Pa explained that several southern states have broken away—seceded—from our Union to protest Mr. Lincoln's victory in the election. Those rebellious states have formed a new nation called the Confederate States of America. Oh, Regina, our Nation has been severed!

My sweet mother always frets whenever one of us is upset, and so she sugared more bread and took it upstairs to my brother. She found his window wide open—Bob had run away! Ma flew downstairs crying out for Pa, and he left at once to search for my brother. Shortly before midnight Pa found Bob sleeping on a bench at the train station, and after much talk he convinced him to come home.

Ever since last night there has been an awful silence in my house, a sad sort of silence that suffocates me. If the Inauguration of President Lincoln could cause so much sorrow in my own family, can you imagine the suffering throughout our Nation? My heart is swollen with fear.

Saturday, March 16

I am glad to learn that you and your dear uncle and aunt are faring well in spirit and health. My family has known happier times, but I myself am faring well.

My brother is still moody and at times angry, but we ignore his bitter words about President Lincoln. Although he agrees with Mr. Lincoln that human bondage is an abomination, Bob resents Mr. Lincoln's interference with states that choose to tolerate slavery. Pa has explained to Bob again and again that President Lincoln must do whatever is necessary to preserve our Union. Bob must suffer deafness at times, for he doesn't seem to hear Pa.

Pa's real estate business may go bankrupt. Now that the future of our country is so uncertain, fewer houses and buildings are being sold. Ma is so worried about money that we are eating boiled oats or boiled potatoes for every meal.

Our being poor irritates Mary—she fears she will never wear a silken hat or ride in a fancy carriage. Ever since her fourteenth birthday last summer, my sister has walked about in a daze, dreaming of Parisian gowns and moonlit walks with beaux who speak of courtship. I wish a gentleman would court my silly sister and take her far, far away, for she is quite perturbed with me. She complains that I, though younger than she, have a beau when she has none. Must I keep reminding Mary that Boudy is my friend, not my beau? For heaven's sake, Regina, I am only thirteen years of age and Boudy is twenty-five!

I must close now—Pa is complaining about our diet of boiled potatoes, so tonight Ma wants me to crush the potatoes and add a little milk and salt. Soupy potatoes will surely taste dreadful, but I suppose any change is welcome.

P.S.—Bob was in fine spirits today, for the Confederacy has chosen a President, a Virginian named Mr. Jefferson Davis. Pa heard that Mr. Davis would rather weed his gardens than play President—let us hope he will weary of Rebellion and return to his flowers.

Wednesday, March 27

You asked so many questions that my hand will weaken with cramps before I satisfy your curiosity! I thought I had described Boudy in my Christmas letter, but perhaps I did not.

To begin with, his name is Elias Cornelius Boudinot, but I have shortened it to Boudy. He is a lawyer and a journalist, and Pa says that his reputation throughout Arkansas is that of an honorable man. I am quite certain that I mentioned in my last letter that Boudy is twelve years older than I—he will be twenty-six on his next birthday.

Regina, I will gladly make you a sketch of Boudy's face and send it within the week, but for now I will describe him to you. Boudy is handsome as only Cherokees are handsome. His hair is night-black, and his dazzling eyes are as dark as onyx beneath eyebrows that arch up like broken arrows. His face appears carved in stone, for his chin is cut square like a block of granite and his cheeks are high and sharp like a cliff's edge.

I know I am describing Boudy as though he were a statue, but at times he has the appearance of one; there are times when he argues so furiously about President Lincoln and states' rights that his face hardens like marble. Boudy quarrels most fiercely with me, for he resents my devotion to Mr. Lincoln! Pa is amused by the fury of our political debates. Indeed, he smiles whenever my defense of Mr. Lincoln causes Boudy to snatch his hat and stride off our front porch without bidding us good night.

I should explain that after such arguments Boudy always returns on the morrow with a tin of candies.

In answer to your frank question about Boudy—yes, I do love him, but only as one loves a close friend or brother. Mary insists that Boudy is smitten with me; she predicts that he is waiting for my fourteenth birthday to profess himself as my suitor. Oh, Regina, I hope not, for I must tell you of the secret hidden deep in my heart. I do love someone—a gentleman named John Rollin Ridge. John is respected here in Arkansas, for he is the son of the famous Cherokee Chief John Ridge.

John Rollin Ridge (isn't his name divine?) closely resembles Boudy, as well he should, for John and Boudy are cousins. Both are handsome with their dark, flashing eyes and their quick smiles, but there is one important difference between them. Whereas Boudy argues and shouts about Mr. Lincoln or the Southern Rebellion, John speaks quietly of birds and souls and clouds.

Next to my pa, John is the kindest, gentlest man I have ever met. He is a poet, you see, a poet of exquisite poems that whisper words of beauty and pain and joy and sorrow and love. John is a journalist by trade, but one day the entire country—no, the entire world—will pay homage to his poetry.

Please don't breathe a word of this to your uncle and aunt, but when I am fourteen I will encourage John to court me. Perhaps on my sixteenth birthday I will even permit him to kiss my hand!

There—my wonderful secret is in your good care, Regina. I dare not tell my sister about my feelings for John because she would be shocked, for you see, dear friend, John is nearly twenty years older than I. His advanced age does not bother me in the least, except that I, a girl not yet a woman, dare not ask if he intends to court me.

Ma and Pa said I may marry after my seventeenth birthday. Oh, if I were seventeen this very moment I would boldly ask John if he loves me as I love him. How slowly years pass for someone as impatient as I am.

I must close now, for Pa and Ma have invited John and

Boudy for an evening of music and readings, and my guitar is sadly out of tune.

Sunday, April 14

Tonight Pa came home from his office with such a pale, worried look about him that Ma made him sit in the rocker by the hearth. Mary and I draped a blanket around his shoulders, and Bob brought him a cup of hot sweetened tea. Pa sat quietly for ever so long as he stared into the flames of the fire, trouble furrowing his brow. When he spoke at last, his voice was low and flat. He said, "Our Nation is at War."

Ma gasped and clutched Pa's hands. My heart pounded so loudly that I barely heard Mary's question, "With whom, Pa, are we at War?"

Pa's eyes reflected great sadness when he answered, "We are at War with ourselves." Oh, Regina, Pa explained that we have entered a civil war, a struggle between our states. Surely this War Against Ourselves is the cruelest kind.

I glanced at Bob and was terrified by what I saw, for in his eyes I saw joy. Pure joy. My brother—the brother I love and thought I knew—welcomes this War wholeheartedly. I prayed fervently that he'd conceal his strange joy as my sister asked Pa how this War began.

Mr. Lincoln hates War, Pa reminded us. It was Jefferson Davis who forced War upon our Nation yesterday morning when his army of rebels fired their cannons at Fort Sumter, South Carolina. Truly, blood stains the hands of that traitor!

Ma's voice trembled as she assured us that the War will end within weeks, but my brother laughed cruelly and said the War will not end until the Confederacy declares Victory. Oh, Regina, when my parents turned and looked at my brother their

sweet faces were etched with sorrow, complete and utter sorrow.

I am so distraught that I had to sit down at once and write to you, my dear, dear friend. I fear this War will destroy all we love—our families, our friends, and our country. I will close now, Regina, for I have a thousand prayers to say on this terribly sad night.

Sunday, April 28

Yesterday I had a nasty row with my brother. Bob was kneeling by the hearth writing the name of our state in the ashes, and when I asked him why, he laughed. He said that Arkansas has seceded from the Union. I was so angry at his wicked lie that I threw a jug of water at the ashes, and much of the water splashed on my brother's face. Ma made me apologize, for she said Bob had not told a falsehood.

It seems rather unbelievable, Regina, that I am living in a Confederate state. How I wish I were back with you at school in Missouri and we could laugh again and forget these troubled times!

Last night I dreamed I was small again, perhaps five or six years of age, and living once more in my beloved Wisconsin. In my dream I stepped outside my house (the very log cabin I was born in), and surrounding me, as far as I could see, were other children—tiny children of the Winnebago tribe. They looked thin. Hungry. As I walked amongst them I placed crusts of bread in their cupped hands, when of a sudden, rain fell, hard and cold, and the children melted away. I stood there, alone and sorrowful, until I noticed towering rocks of purple and blue and grey twisted into odd yet beautiful shapes. My hands were ungloved, and using my bare fingers, I touched and pushed and cut the rocks until they changed into statues of the

Indian children. The statues grew so lifelike that my loneliness and sadness disappeared.

When I awoke I remembered my dream and opening my keepsake box I looked at the small rocks I had collected while living in Wisconsin. Do you remember the purple and grey and black rocks I once showed you? Whenever I feel unhappy or frightened I simply touch my rocks, and their textures and pretty colors never fail to comfort me. How I wish my dream could come true and I could take rocks and sculpt them into the Indian children I once played with and loved!

I am glad to learn that you take such pleasure in your French lessons. I wish Ma and Pa still had money so that I could continue my schooling. I dearly miss you and our days in the Academy at Christian College. Do you remember how Melissa Turnby and Sarah Goodall hated their practice sessions on the harp and harpsichord and how they'd let us climb through the window and take their turns while they sat in the corner playing cards? Do you remember the beautiful oak tree we sat in while we read Mr. Shakespeare's sonnets? Do you remember the joy we took sitting for hours at the easels? How I miss painting, but we can't afford paint and brushes (Pa hasn't sold a house in months).

I am pleased that you liked my sketches of Boudy and John Rollin Ridge (I do so love the sound of John's name), and I am especially pleased that you found both gentlemen as handsome as I do.

Of late, I have seen neither Boudy nor John, for there is much commotion here at Fort Smith since the declaration of War. Pa said that our agitation here is nothing compared to the turmoil in the Southern seaport states now that President Lincoln has blocked their ports—imagine, Regina, if you lived in the South, you couldn't buy French candy or books of poetry from

England or wool from Ireland to knit your socks.

Yesterday I found Mary crying because a blemish spotted her chin and she feared that she was scarred for life. My silly sister doesn't realize that if she had a thousand blemishes and warts she would still be beautiful. When I finish the sketch I am secretly making of her, I'll show her the image as proof of her beauty. (If I had paint I'd color the sketch, for Mary's hair is still the color of winter corn and her eyes are as blue as a summer sky.) Truly, I believe that gentlemen never call on my sister because they fear that someone as exquisite as she would reject their offers of matrimony.

I must close now, as Ma is calling us for supper. Boiled potatoes, of course! When I feel tempted to complain I remember the starving Indian families we often fed during our winters in Wisconsin.

Friday, June 28

The other day Pa came home carrying a wooden box of papers and books. He placed the box on the mantel, and turning to Bob and Mary and me, he said, "Your mother and I are as tired of potatoes for breakfast, dinner, and supper as you are." Oh, Regina, Pa then told us the most shocking news—he has sold his business! In two days we will move to our Nation's capital city, Washington, D.C.

Ma explained that she and Pa had decided to resettle there because the War has opened hundreds of government jobs. Pa hopes to find work again as a surveyor or perhaps as a cartographer. (If Missouri's bitter weather hadn't caused Pa's rheumatism he would never have retired from the government and tried to sell real estate here in Arkansas, for he enjoyed drawing maps.)

Mary, Bob, and I were astonished, to say the least. Bob is excited about the move because he heard there are important Confederate sympathizers in Washington. Mary is practically dancing about, for she dreams that the Capital will be crowded with rich gentlemen searching desperately for wives. For myself, I am torn, Regina, between excitement about living in a large city and sorrow about leaving John Rollin Ridge and Boudy. Especially now.

Last night Pa told them that we were leaving Fort Smith forever. Boudy was keenly disappointed and said so, but John said nothing, nothing at all, which tore at my heart. Then he glanced my way and I saw that his eyes were shadowed with grief. I knew in that moment that he loves me as I love him.

While they were bidding us good night, I said to John, "You have written some beautiful poems. I want you to write one for me as a parting gift which I shall keep always." He smiled so sadly, so sweetly, and taking hold of his reins, he mounted his horse and galloped off into the darkness.

Last night I pressed my face deep into my pillow and cried myself to sleep.

This morning, as I was boiling oats for our breakfast, there came a quick knock at the door. John stood on our back step with a brown envelope in his hand. Inside the envelope, on a piece of onionskin paper, was a poem that he wrote for me last night.

> I love thee, as the soaring bird
> The bright blue morning, when he sings,
> In circling melodies,
> With Heaven's sweet sunlight on his wings.

I love thee, as the mariner,
Far driven o'er a stormy sea,
The silver rising star
Which tells him where his home may be.

I love thee as the billows love
In tropic lands the pearly shore;
They come and go
With answering kisses evermore!

I love thee. Ever, ever shall
Thine eyes' dark, glorious light
Dwell in my soul,
Illumining its deeps of night.

Regina, after I read John's poem I looked up and found he had gone. Oh, why did he leave without bidding me farewell? How I wish I could see him once again, but somehow I know I never will.

Tonight my pillow will again be wetted by my tears, for tomorrow the morning train will take me far away from my Poet, John.

Saturday, June 29

This train journey has just begun, and yet with each passing mile my old home in Fort Smith seems another world away. Ahead of me lies an unknown world, my new home in Washington, D.C.

Oh, Regina, what will my life there be like? I imagine sophisticated people of education and culture. I imagine lovely parks of roses and marble fountains and benches where I will sit one day and speak with an admirer. I imagine grand homes with graceful drives and carriages pulled by handsome white horses.

I am glad I own an imagination, for when I weary of looking out the window at the towns and hills and valleys rushing by, I close my eyes and dream of my future home. I try not to think too much about Fort Smith, for that is where I left behind John Rollin Ridge and Boudy.

I have only one envelope and so I will continue to add to this letter until I find a Post Office along our journey to the north and east.

Sunday, June 30

This train is quite uncomfortable. The passengers sit close together on benches that are rather hard. (Poor Mary, determined to sit upright as a proper lady should, complains that her back aches terribly.) The haze of tobacco smoke chokes me and the wind flitting through the window chills me. The noise of the engine makes conversation difficult but not impossible, if one concentrates on what is being said. In spite of our discomfort we are grateful that Pa was able to sell his business or we would probably be walking to Washington, D.C.

Pa told us that trains such as this one will prove important during the War, for they will speed soldiers and cannons and even horses to battles and afterwards carry the wounded to hospitals and the able to other battles. Pa said that the North controls thousands and thousands of miles of railroads, which caused my brother laughter—wicked laughter—for he said that Confederate Marauders will tear up Northern tracks and wreck Union trains.

Ma was clearly annoyed with my brother, for she is fearful of Confederate Marauders. Throughout our passage in Missouri she kept a fearful look out her window, for she worried that the villainous Confederate William Clarke Quantrill and his gang of Marauders would gallop after our train and fire their pistols into our windows. I am happy to report that we passed through the state without harm.

Monday, July 1
(Written somewhere in the state of Ohio)

The hours pass slowly, for I am not accustomed to sitting still for so long. I thirst all the time, for there is a fine dust that dances in the air and dries out my throat. I am constantly hungry, too (Ma said I may be growing, Regina, which would be wonderful, for I am still terribly short). My face feels grimy and my hair feels soiled from the dirt and smoke clouding the air in this carriage. (I wish Pa and Ma would allow me to cut my hair—it is heavy and long and bothersome.)

The rocking movement of the train is lulling me to sleep. I shall write again tomorrow.

Tuesday, July 2

Tomorrow has come, Regina, and with it much excitement. Last night we stopped at a town for water and coal. While we were there a cool summer rain brought on one of Pa's attacks of rheumatism, and no sooner had we boarded the train again than Pa collapsed in his seat. An army doctor and three wounded soldiers also boarded the train with us. Noting Pa's suffering, the doctor arranged to seat himself and the soldiers across the aisle from us. The doctor attended Pa with great solicitude and then gave him a draught of sour-smelling syrup that caused Pa to fall into a much-needed sleep.

While Pa was sleeping Ma thanked the doctor for his help

and he kindly refused her offer of payment. In the charming, foreign accent of the Germans, he introduced himself as Dr. Herbert Heimler. The good doctor told us that he was traveling to an army hospital in Washington, D.C., to volunteer as a surgeon for wounded soldiers.

Boldly I asked about the soldiers he accompanied, and in a lowered voice he explained that they had been wounded during a skirmish and he had offered to escort them to hospitals in Washington.

Two of the soldiers, their heads wrapped in bandages, sat in the seat behind Dr. Heimler. The other soldier slept fitfully by the doctor's side. Often I stole glances at the sleeping soldier (I had a clear view of his face), and I soon decided that he was a boy, not a man. It was difficult to tell, though, for he had been carried onto the train wrapped in a blanket and only his shoes and head were revealed. Many passengers noticed that he was shivering violently and that his cheeks were scarlet red, but the doctor assured everyone that the soldier's fever was caused by his infected wounds and not from a deadly disease such as measles. I wondered what his wounds were, but I dared not ask the doctor for fear he might think me forward. I waited until Dr. Heimler had drifted off to sleep to begin my study of the soldier.

Upon careful study I was convinced that he was indeed only a boy. His hair was yellow like sun-bleached lemons, but his thick brows and lashes were almost black. Small honey-colored freckles were scattered over the bridge of his perfectly straight nose and across his rounded cheeks. Except for his wide chin, the chin of a man of strength, his face was the face of a boy. I stared at him and wondered what his name was and where he once lived and if he had a family and a sweetheart, but mostly I wondered what terrible injuries were hidden beneath the blanket that could cause his cheeks to burn with fever.

At one point last night, when everyone slept but me, the soldier stirred. Under the moon's bright light I saw his eyelids flicker open. He blinked a few times, rustled the blanket, and looked about the carriage. Seeing that I watched him, he asked, "Where am I?"

I told him and he nodded by way of reply and closed his eyes again. After a while he reopened his eyes (his eyes were dark, the color of mahogany, and they were glazed with the fever). "Who are you?" he asked me in a voice that sounded both young and old. I gave him my name and he closed his eyes and slept.

Early this morning, before dawn, the soldier fully awoke. His cheeks were no longer red and fevered and his eyes shone clear. He greeted me with a smile and remembered my name, which flattered me. His name was James Kilmar and I soon had the answers to my questions. I learned that he was from the city of Annapolis, Maryland, and though he had no sweetheart he dearly loved his mother, a widow.

Shyly I commented that he didn't look old enough to serve as a soldier, and he confided that he hasn't seen his eighteenth year. He admitted with equal shyness that he was only fourteen years of age—only a year older than you and I, Regina!

James said he knew when he enlisted that he would have to swear an oath that he was "over eighteen years of age," and so he wrote the number "18" inside his shoes. Then, when he took the oath, he truthfully pledged that he was "over" eighteen. James told me that he has met many boys his own age who have also lied about their age in order to fight for our country. Indeed, he once met a boy, not yet nine years of age, serving as a drummer for a unit from Delaware!

In truth, we spoke little about the War, but we spoke endlessly about music.

I told him about the Indians I had trained on the guitar in Wisconsin, about how we formed a band and performed at weddings and church socials. I told him of my study of the harp, harpsichord, and banjo at Christian College and how I took voice lessons and wrote music (I even told him that your uncle, as President of our Academy, had chosen one of my musical compositions for a school song). And I told him about John Rollin Ridge's romantic poem that I shall set to music.

In turn, James told me about his voice, said to have operatic quality, and about his acceptance at age twelve to the Peabody Conservatory of Music in Baltimore City. He told me that in addition to training his voice he studied Italian, German, and French so as to sing the operas written in those languages. He told me that he had also discovered the trumpet, quite by accident, and quickly mastered the instrument (his heart's dream is to play trumpet in orchestras that tour the grand salons and theatres of America and Europe). And he told me how he had run away from the Conservatory to enlist as a bugler in Mr. Lincoln's army.

We told each other much about ourselves. Perhaps if someone had eavesdropped they would have thought that James and I were boasting about our musical achievements! We were not, Regina—we were merely sharing our joy of music.

At one point, as I mentioned that I missed the harp, I asked if he grew impatient to play his trumpet again. The smile vanished from his wood-brown eyes and he said, in a low voice, "I will never play the trumpet again."

His answer puzzled me, but before I could query why, he asked me to open the satchel at his feet. Inside was a composition book and on the first page was a piece of music he had written for his mother. At James's direction I held up the book and he whistled the tune. It was lovely, Regina, sweet and spirited.

I blurted out, "Although you have abandoned the trumpet, you still have your voice … Add words to your composition and upon your return home you could sing your song to your mother."

My suggestion clearly pained him. His face crumpling with agony, he whispered that his mother had had grand hopes for him at the Conservatory but his professors would never welcome him back. And he said that he couldn't bear to see disappointment darken his mother's eyes and so he would never see her again—he believes she would be happier if she believed him to be dead.

James's puzzling words stabbed me with sorrow, but sensing that he wanted no further questioning, I did not ask why he couldn't return to his school of music and thus to his beloved mother.

By mid-morning James's fever had returned, but the doctor gave him a draught that brought him sleep. In his sleep James must have felt pain, for he moved about restlessly, fitfully. I watched over him, worried by his fever and disturbed by what he had told me, and as I watched, his blanket fell to the floor.

James had no hands. Two flattened bandages were pinned to the cuffs of his sleeves. The bandages were spotted with his red blood. My throat tightened as I stared at those dreadful clumps of bandage. No hands. No hands to hold his trumpet. No hands to embrace his mother. No hands, Regina. No hands.

I ran to the back of the train and leaning through the open door I became ill. Ma came to me, as did Dr. Heimler. He gave me a potion to calm my stomach, and while Ma held me in her arms, he told us about James and other boys like him who pretend to be men so as to serve as buglers for our army.

During battles, he said, there is much smoke and noise and thus much confusion, so soldiers listen to the bugles. Different musical notes tell the soldiers when to advance right or left and when to attack or retreat to safety. The bugle boys are targets during battles, for only death can silence their horns.

The doctor arranged bed pallets in the mail car, and before the wounded soldiers were carried out, I bade James farewell. I never revealed to him that I had discovered his terrible secret, for I sensed that he was ashamed of his wounds.

How I wish I could find Mrs. Kilmar! James mentioned that she still lives in Annapolis, a town near Washington. How sad that only a few hours, a few miles, will separate James from the mother he loves so dearly. I pity his mother, too, for she will never see her son again or hear his beautiful song. Oh, Regina, its melody will haunt me forever.

Pa said there is a Post Office at our next stop, Baltimore City, Maryland, so I will finally close this long letter. My next letter will be posted from my new home in Washington, D.C.— until then, dear friend, know that you are in my daily thoughts and prayers.

Thursday, July 4

I can hardly believe that I am writing this letter in our Nation's capital city!

Early this morning, after the break of day, our train pulled into a station that appeared so shabby that I refused at first to believe we had reached Washington, D.C. I had imagined an elegant station befitting our capital, but I soon learned that this city is nothing like the one in my imagination.

We stood there on that filthy, debris-strewn platform and around us were hundreds and hundreds of soldiers—soldiers sleeping on blankets, soldiers sitting around campfires, soldiers with blood-caked bandages, soldiers writing letters or reading, soldiers eating and smoking—and all of their tired faces were marked by the grime and horror of War.

Some of the soldiers looked our way, curious I suppose, but most paid us little heed. I heard much snoring and coughing, and I smelled urine and vomit and whiskey. Mary held her kerchief against her nose, but I marched through the throngs of men. I didn't mind their rude noises or nasty odors, for I was filled with pride for our brave soldiers.

Outside the station my family and I stared in dismay at the street before us. It was crowded with horses and carriages and large army wagons carrying soldiers, cannons, hay, piles of saddles, and sacks of flour and potatoes. Pa took one look at the thundering hooves and the rumbling wheels and decided to hire a wagon to take us to the boarding house. Within the hour we were loading our few cases onto a black wagon drawn by a sweet horse.

As we drove away from the station we traveled down streets that were edged with houses and buildings and tents and mansions and stables. The streets seemed endless and the city was a confusing maze. I hadn't realized that Washington would be so large, but Pa explained that nearly sixty-six thousand people live here. Imagine, Regina, sixty-six thousand people! Pa said that the number grows every day as hundreds of men arrive to enlist in our army and navy.

The boarding house wasn't far from the station, but our passage was slow, for the poor horse had to pull our wagon through thick mud, around deep holes, and through packs of fat, grunting pigs rooting in rubbish. Some of the streets were cobbled with uneven brick, and some were like rivers of soft mud, but all were lined with soldiers sleeping on blankets or sitting on the ground.

At one corner, while we waited as a flock of ducks scattered across the street, we saw a soldier sitting with his back to a wall. He stared at us for a long moment and then began to shake as though struck by spasms. After a spell he grew still, his eyes closed, and he slumped sideways. Regina, that poor, poor man died alone on that soiled street and there was nothing we could do to help him. Nor could we stop and help the other wounded soldiers. We passed by men with eyes grim with agony, clothes dark with blood, faces red with fever, and there was nothing we could do. Nothing. Why weren't those wretched men in hospitals? After a while I shut my eyes against their misery. I thought, if this suffering is present at the beginning of this War when few skirmishes have been fought, what miseries await us by War's end?

All at once I understood, Regina, that those soldiers believe in Mr. Lincoln and his War to reunite our Nation. I understood that they believe passionately enough to suffer pain and risk death. Understanding swelled my heart with such pride and love that I feared my heart might burst. I knew then that I couldn't hide selfishly from their suffering. My eyes flew open. I looked at the faces of our soldiers and breathed in the smells of burnt cabbage and gangrenous wounds and vomit and death and listened to their moans of pain. And I told myself that like those soldiers I, too, will commit myself to the struggle for our Nation's reunification. How I will help Mr. Lincoln and his Great Cause I cannot yet determine, but I will. I swear this,

Regina. Somehow I will help Mr. Lincoln.

On Pennsylvania Avenue our horse became skittish when a cart of caged chickens broke a wheel and blocked our path. The driver of our wagon yanked on his reins and jumped down to calm his horse before guiding him around the chicken cart. Suddenly he paused and stared.

Puzzled, I turned to where he looked and saw a tall man walking towards us. He looked like an ordinary man except that he was rather tall—the towering stovepipe hat he wore only added to his unusual height. He was dressed in a dark suit, as seems to be the custom in the city, but about his rounded shoulders was wrapped a white shawl. Oh, Regina, that man was no ordinary man. He was our beloved President, Abraham Lincoln.

I stood up slowly, very slowly, as though sudden movement might burst the illusion like a fragile bubble. But he was no illusion. He came closer and closer until I clearly saw the coarseness of his face, the darkness of his beard, the slope of his shoulders as though he bore a burden on his back, and the measured stride of his long legs. He came even closer and closer and then my happy heart felt troubled, for I saw the lines of sadness on his face. Deep, deep lines of sadness that made my eyes tear. Ma noticed my distress and pulled me down beside her and asked why I wept.

I could not speak. I just sat there, cradled in Ma's arms, crying softly for that Solitary Man passing by our wagon. And as I watched Mr. Lincoln walk up the street, I knew that he was unmindful of the mud and rubbish, for I knew with equal certainty that his mind dwelt on our Nation's troubles.

Before I realized it, our wagon was under way again. After a while we passed onto an unpaved street to the boarding house where we are lodging until Pa and Ma find us a home of our own.

This boarding house is owned by a brisk little widow with nine cats to whom she speaks as one speaks to children. At present we are her only boarders (a family from France recently moved out). Mary and I are sharing the front room, which has a single bed (the mattress smells as though it is stuffed with stinkweed), a chair, and a table. I am seated at that table now as I write to you, my dear friend.

Tomorrow Pa is to be given an interview at the War Department (his expert surveys of western Missouri are still valued by our government, so Ma has much hope that Pa will secure immediate employment). After his interview we shall walk about the city to look for a small house.

I will close now, for I am anxious to take out John Rollin Ridge's poem and set his words to music. Then, whenever I think fondly of my Dear Poet, I will play my guitar and sing the words he penned just for me.

P.S.—It doesn't seem fair that our Nation is separated on her birthday.

Monday, July 22

As usual, I have much to tell you. Pa has been commissioned as a half-day cartographer for the War Department, and Ma found us a narrow brick house with a kitchen, parlor, and dining room on the first floor and three small bedrooms on the second (thankfully Pa had enough money left over from the sale of his business). Our new address is No. 325 North B Street, Capitol Hill, Washington, D.C.

I have claimed the top floor, the attic, for my bedroom, for there is a long row of windows that allows perfect light for sketching and painting. (Pa surprised me with a gift of paper, brushes, and eight tins of paint!) My wonderful attic is simply furnished with a bed, a clothing cupboard, a chair and large desk, and a pretty rug made of twisted rags. Against one wall is a wide bookcase on which I have arranged my rock collection and sketches, my music sheets and guitar.

My windows look down on the city of Washington. Since yesterday night I have looked down upon the Traffic of War—when you finish this letter you'll understand the meaning of those words.

Until yesterday, Mary was being courted by a gentleman named Roger Whittman, the son of the banker who arranged a loan for my parents to properly furnish our house. Bob wondered why a rich man's son would court our sister, but I reminded him that she is as sweet as she is beautiful. Personally, though, I don't know why Mary allowed Mr. Whittman to call on her, for he has watery eyes, a weak mouth, and no chin and he stands as stiff as a board. Roger Whittman's personality is that of a milkweed—he has no opinion about the War or anything of importance.

This is what happened, Regina. Roger had invited my sister to picnic with him and his society friends yesterday in the countryside of Virginia, at a spot near Manassas. Mary and Roger's carriage left here at dawn because Manassas is nearly twenty-five miles away and they wished to arrive in time for the luncheon. Pa was against Mary's going, but Ma gave her blessing, for I suspect she had a hope that Roger might propose marriage.

Late last night came Mary's soft knock at our door. My sister stood there alone with her hair disheveled, her gown splattered with mud, and her face smudged by dirt and tears. As Ma's eyes widened in horror, Pa demanded to know what Roger had done to my poor sister.

"He deserted me!" Mary cried out. "I will never speak to that coward again."

Mary dropped into Pa's rocker, and after we had given her a cup of mint tea to calm her nerves she told us about her adventure. The luncheon at Manassas was elegant—the ladies and gentlemen sipped lemonade from crystal glasses and ate cucumber sandwiches off china plates. But Mary was hardly comfortable, for the sun burned down on that field of dead grasses, and noisy insects buzzed over a nearby stream, named the Bull Run. Indeed, she complained to us that the picnic lacked romance.

Mary became a bit alarmed when she learned that a few miles away the Federal army was fighting the Confederate army. Although she heard the soft booms of cannons and the popping of muskets, she wasn't overly frightened, for Roger convinced her that the Union would win the battle and thus end the War.

Roger was wrong. The Union was defeated. As dusk reddened the sky, my sister and the other ladies packed the empty baskets for the drive back to Washington while a grim parade of defeated soldiers walked past. All at once cannons fired upon them, and everyone, including my sister, ran hysterically towards a bridge. But the bridge was blocked by dead horses and Mary knew she lacked the nerve to climb over them, so she looked around for Roger's carriage. Though he saw her, he whipped his horses into a frenzy and drove off through the stream of water. Screaming, Mary ran after him, but that coward never once looked back. Fortunately, a kindly soldier, pitying my poor sister, picked her up and threw her into the passing carriage of a congressman and his wife.

After my sister had sobbed out her story, Pa slipped out of the house while Ma and I tucked Mary into bed. A while later

Pa arrived home with frightful news. My sister had not exaggerated, Regina. The battle had been bloody. Hundreds of our soldiers were killed, hundreds captured, and thousands horribly wounded.

Thence came my remark that the Traffic of War is passing below my attic windows. Last night and into this morning's hours I have watched the return of our soldiers from the battle they now call Bull Run. Some walk slowly, their heads and shoulders rounded by weariness. Others limp down the street, their uniforms ragged and bloodied, their faces blackened by dirt and smoke. Still others are half-dragged, half-carried by their comrades and the citizens of this city. And those who are nearly dead pass by on wagons that serve as crowded ambulances. Even as I finish this letter the procession of defeated men, the Traffic of War, continues.

Regina, I doubt that this War will end as quickly as Ma promised.

Monday, August 12

Several weeks ago Pa was gravely ill. The doctor determined that his illness was wrought from fatigue, for although he was hired to work half days, he often worked twelve-hour days to earn extra money. At Ma's insistence he now works only four hours a day. Pa worried that the reduction in his salary would bring about hardship, but Bob has been hired to clean out stables and there is money enough for food.

For myself I am delighted each noon hour when I hear Pa's step at our door. I always have a tray prepared with hot broth, honeyed bread, and tea, and we sit together talking in the parlor while we eat. Our hour alone is a peaceful time for Pa and me—Mary is usually upstairs practicing dance steps with a broom, and Ma is most often in the kitchen baking our daily bread. With my brother at work most days now, Pa and I are spared Bob's loud criticisms of Mr. Lincoln.

During our hour together we often discuss this terrible War. How I love my pa—he never laughs at my opinions and he listens to me as though my comments are quite sensible.

Today Pa brought inside a letter from Boudy. He waited patiently while I read it to myself, and then, blinded by tears, I handed the letter back to Pa so that he, too, could read the dreadful news—Boudy has enlisted in the Confederate Army.

Regina, my heart has shattered like glass struck by a stone. I feel betrayed—betrayed by a beloved friend who has turned against our country—betrayed by my beloved Boudy, who has turned against me.

Pa made me sit in Ma's chair, and he took down her shawl and wrapped it around my shoulders. Then he sat in silence until my tears were spent before he said, "Vinnie, you believe strongly in our Union's struggle—just as strongly as Boudy believes in the struggle of the Confederacy."

I wanted Pa to understand my disappointment in Boudy, so I asked him what he would do if my brother, Bob, enlisted in the Confederate Army.

Pa didn't answer me. I began to wonder if he had even heard me, but then in a quiet voice he said, "I would pray for Bob to return from the War unharmed."

For a long while Pa and I sat without speaking. I thought about Boudy and I believe Pa thought about my brother, for a sad silence surrounded us both.

I will close now, Regina, for I have promised to scrub the kitchen floor. (I spilled a crock of honey, and although I wiped up the mess, Ma's shoes are still sticking to the floor.)

P.S.—Please write more about Mr. Edward Hamilton. How fortunate for your uncle to have found in Mr. Hamilton a Scientist for the Academy. And how fortunate for you, Regina, to have found in Mr. Hamilton a gentleman of pleasant company!

Tuesday, September 24

I had to write you at once to thank you for the lovely handkerchief. No one can embroider roses more delicately, Regina. How I admire your skill with a needle—I fear that I am more skilled at collecting rocks than I am at stitching fine cloth.

And thank you, too, for the book of poems. I had heard of the Englishman John Keats, but I had never happened upon a collection of his poetry. How tragic that he died before he married, and at such a youthful age. Tuberculosis is a horrid disease to have stolen such a fine poet from our world.

How very strange it feels to have reached my fourteenth year! I feel disappointed in myself, as though I should have done something of importance by now. But I must close now, for my family awaits downstairs to surprise me with my birthday supper.

P.S.—I heartily agree with you, Regina—surely your Mr. Hamilton is smitten with you. And no wonder, dear friend, for you are as lovely as the roses you embroider.

Tuesday, October 8

Last night while my parents, my sister, and I slept, my brother slipped out of the house, having pinned a brief letter of farewell to his pillow. He wrote that he must follow his conscience—he has run away to join the Confederate Army.

Oh, Regina, I am numb with grief. I knew of course that my brother sympathized with the Confederacy, but I had hoped he'd be content to stay home until this Conflict between our States is over.

Pa and Ma are at the train station hoping to find him and bring him home. Mary is downstairs weeping, and I sit here before my attic windows searching the street below, praying that I spy my brother's sweet face.

I am confused, Regina. My hope is for the Union to succeed in this Struggle for Reunification, but that struggle will mean the deaths of many Confederate soldiers. Am I thus hoping for the death of my own brother? Or do I callously hope that the brother of someone unknown to me dies in his place?

P.S.—I pray that the Confederacy rejects Bob—after all, he is only sixteen years of age! Then again, James Kilmar joined our Federal army at fourteen years. Undoubtedly the Confederate Army is equally eager to enlist boys and pretend they are men.

Wednesday, November 27

It has been weeks since Bob ran away, and we have not received a single letter from him. My poor mother haunts our letter-box and Pa sits for hours by the hearth just staring into the fire. I am afraid that Joy will evade my parents' hearts until they receive word.

Pa was ill again last week, but only for two days. Now that he works half days at his office he is less fatigued and thus his recoveries are quicker.

Several mornings ago, Ma confided in my sister and me her worries about our finances (Pa's medicines are expensive and we still owe the doctor for his last visit). Ma depended on Bob's salary to help pay our bills, and now his absence leads us towards the poverty we knew in Arkansas. She is determined to find a way to earn some money, but she asked us not to tell Pa—she fears he'd work longer hours again, despite the danger to his health.

On hearing Ma's worries, my sister asked for permission to find a job, but Ma smiled and gently said no. Stubbornly my sister pleaded with Ma. When Ma finally agreed, with reluctance, Mary dashed happily through the front door before Ma could change her mind.

That very day Mary found a job at a land office. She works six hours every day except Sunday. My sister is quite pleased with her position, for she is proud that her salary can help our parents. And she is delighted by the many gentlemen who stop by her office and pause, overlong, to speak with her.

Regina, I wrote to you about the anguish that Boudy's enlistment in the Confederate Army has caused me. Heeding Pa's good advice I wrote Boudy a letter in which I carefully avoided harsh criticism. In mild language I protested his decision to take up weapons against our Union, but I did not condemn his allegiance to the Confederacy. And yet, though I wrote soft words, Boudy has not answered my letter. Oddly, his refusal to write me distresses me more than I could have imagined. Not a day goes by that I don't think about him and my brother, Bob, and wonder where they are and if they are well.

I often think of John Rollin Ridge, too, although he has never written me. Ma said I must not be the first to write or John would think me forward—surely he has not forgotten me!

Today, when Pa and I spent our quiet hour together at noon, we spoke about a general named George McClellan. Pa dislikes him with a passion. I gave Pa my opinion that General McClellan always looks rather striking with his handsome face and immaculate uniform and shiny boots as he leads his army in parades around Washington. Pa smiled at me and said that our Nation needs a general with scuffed boots and soiled hands who can lead us into battle.

I must close now. Pa's oldest friend, Senator Edmund Ross, from the state of Kansas, is coming for tea. Ma wants me to bake raisin scones, the senator's favorite bread. Senator Ross visits my family often, for his wife and children stayed behind in Kansas and he misses the gathering of a family. You would enjoy meeting this fine gentleman, Regina. He is considerate and intelligent and tells the most marvelous stories about the ladies and gentlemen of Washington Society. Ma, who despises gossip, pretends that she disapproves of his colorful stories, but I've noticed that when he speaks, my mother hides small smiles behind her teacup.

P.S.—Ma is making me a beautiful frock for my Christmas present. She took one of Mary's old dresses and is adding bits of lace and cream-colored ribbons. Ma stitches at night when she thinks I am asleep, but often, after she goes downstairs to sit with Pa by the fire, I tiptoe into her bedroom and peek at her handiwork.

I wish I wore hoops like my sister, but Ma said I must wear petticoats until I am older. How lovely it will be when I can finally cast off those heavy garments—this past summer the weather here was so hot and sticky that I nearly melted.

Wednesday, December 25

Another Christmas Day has come and gone. I trust that your holiday has been splendid and merry.

My family received a most precious gift—a long letter from my brother! Bob is well and proud of his decision to support the Confederacy. For the time being he is camped near the Confederate capital of Richmond, Virginia (mere hours from Washington). Bob wrote that he met President Jefferson Davis and was struck by his uncanny resemblance to President

Lincoln. What an odd coincidence, Regina, that the two Presidents should look as though they were brothers.

The dress Ma made me fits perfectly. I wish I could have been genuinely surprised, but I must confess that I even tried it on one day while Ma was out walking. Ma says the dress looks better on me than it ever did on Mary, for the green complements the brown in my eyes and hair. Pa gave me new strings for my guitar and Mary gave me velvet ribbons to wear with my beautiful dress (my sister loved the sketch I made of her, but she still doubts her beauty).

Senator Ross came for Christmas supper. Pa discovered quite by accident that his good friend has been living in his congressional office, sleeping on his desk at night. There are no vacancies in this entire city, which is the reason Senator Ross's family stayed behind in Kansas. Pa, ever kind to his friends, has invited the senator to make use of Bob's bedroom during his absence. Senator Ross accepted Pa's invitation immediately but graciously insisted that he will pay for room and board. I could tell that Ma was relieved, for she worries constantly about money (the cost of food and medicine seems to increase each day).

Christmas supper was a festive meal of roasted goose and cranberries. Senator Ross surprised us with a gift of French chocolates stuffed with strawberry cream.

While we ate our supper, the only topic of discussion was General McClellan. Senator Ross told us that Mr. Lincoln has lost patience with his general and has ordered him to march his army into battle. Pa was delighted by the news.

I will close now by wishing you and your dear uncle and aunt a Blessed New Year.

1862

Sunday, January 26

My dear friend Regina,

I had to reply at once to your letter about your remarkable gentleman, Mr. Edward Hamilton. Your description of him as a scholar, philosopher, scientist, writer, musician, theologian, and sportsman prompts me to call him a modern Renaissance Man—no wonder you are in love with him.

Please write more about this interesting game of baseball that Mr. Hamilton plays. Can he honestly take a thin stick and hit a ball clear across the Academy's green? Pa says that baseball has been played in America since he was a boy, but he believes there is growing interest in the sport, especially amongst the soldiers. Perhaps that curious game offers them relief from the boredom of General McClellan's endless drills of marching back and forth. Regina, do you suppose girls could ever learn how to play this game?

Later today Mary and I are going for a walk. We enjoy our outings in spite of the cold weather, because we never know whom we might spot. A few days ago we saw Mr. Lincoln and his younger sons, Willie and Tad, strolling down our street. Tad was costumed in a soldier's uniform cut to his size. He carried a wooden rifle over one shoulder and marched in front of his father as though guarding him. Willie walked close beside his father, for they were deep in conversation.

Senator Ross often entertains my family with amusing stories about Tad and Willie. Those two boys fill the White House with noise from dawn to dusk as they romp and scream and tumble through the rooms like wild monkeys. The noise bothers everyone except Mr. and Mrs. Lincoln. Indeed, Mr. Lincoln finds peace in all that chaos, for his sons' antics and pranks lift his spirits. Senator Ross said that when Mr. Lincoln's laughter echoes down the halls of the White House, those who understand the President know that he has discovered renewed strength and calmness to return to the problems and decisions and horrors of War.

Tad is eight years of age, I believe. He is the dark-haired, dark-eyed son you may have seen imaged in your newspaper. Twice now, Mary and I have seen him walking with his father. My sister regards Tad as grotesque because of his coarse features and his baggy pants that button up to his waist. I wouldn't use a word as harsh as that, for I recognize in Tad a resemblance to our wonderful President. I see in Tad's face honesty, goodness, and intelligence, and yet I will admit that his is not the face of a cherub.

Even though Senator Ross's tales prove that Tad is a mischievous scamp, they also reveal his devotion to his parents. Often Tad will raid the White House gardens to gather bouquets for his mother, and he sits for hours under his father's chair, often falling asleep with his head on Mr. Lincoln's slippered foot. What a marvelous mix of devil and angel Tad seems! I suppose he is merely a marvelous boy.

Willie is eleven years of age. He, too, is a prankster, but he has enough good sense to stop his brother from playing jests that are too dangerous. My sister thinks Willie the more handsome of the two brothers with his blue eyes and light brown hair. He resembles in coloring his pretty mother, but Senator Ross said that Willie also resembles his father, for he has inherited his father's kind heart and clever mind.

It is said that Willie is especially close to his mother (he calls himself "Mother's boy"), but Senator Ross observed that a special bond exists between the kind, gentle Willie and his quiet, gentle father. I agree with the senator, for each time I spot

Willie on the street, I am struck by the way he walks beside his father as though he were his shadow.

P.S.—Washington is afire with the news that President Lincoln is angered by General McClellan's refusal to lead his army into battle. Senator Ross overheard Mr. Lincoln say that the General's delay is killing us.

Wednesday, February 12

This evening Senator Ross attended an elaborate Entertainment at the White House. He arrived home wearing a face of such weariness that Pa insisted that he take the chair nearest the fire and Ma added mint to his tea. Quietly my family gathered in chairs around him to hear about the event.

It was a grand affair, Senator Ross told us, crowded with politicians, military officers, foreign dignitaries, and the gentlemen and ladies of Washington Society. He described the elegance of the gathering: the candlelight on the crystal and silver trays, the flowers strewn around lanterns, the jewel-colored gowns of the ladies, the resplendent attire of the gentlemen, and the rousing music of the Marine Band.

He smiled as he spoke, but as he fell silent the smile vanished from his face. Puzzled, I asked how a festive occasion could darken his heart.

Senator Ross put down his cup. Then, in a low voice, he told us that he sensed that the Lincolns were sorely troubled tonight. Watching them, he noticed how often Mrs. Lincoln slipped upstairs to their family's rooms, and upon each return she caught her husband's eye and shook her head slightly, sadly. Senator Ross questioned a servant and learned the cause of the Lincolns' distress—one of their sons, Willie, is dangerously ill with Fever.

Oh, Regina, when he spoke that child's name a needle pricked at my heart. Tonight I shall pray for Willie.

Sunday, February 16

Why does February refuse to end? These past days have crept by so slowly that they are mistook for centuries. Perhaps time creeps because Willie Lincoln's illness does not end.

When the newspaper described Willie as "hopelessly ill," Senator Ross went immediately to the Lincolns' home to inquire about their son. He learned that Willie suffers from the dreaded disease Typhoid, which explains why his dangerous fever has lingered so long. The senator also learned that Willie's breathing is labored, as though the very air chokes him.

The senator did not speak to Mrs. Lincoln, for she has hardly left her son's bedside since the fever fell upon him. While Willie sleeps she washes the fever waters from his brow, and when he wakes she feeds him spoonfuls of water or soup.

Oh, Regina, Willie is so very young—three years younger than you and I. How sad to think of his mother watching, helplessly, like a bird who must watch as her chick slips from beneath her wing and plunges into the abyss.

Thursday, February 20

I write this note in the quiet of my attic room. Darkness has fallen and shadows touch this very paper that I write upon. And yet, in spite of the darkness, I must write to you, Regina, for my heart will burst if I don't release my sadness through these words I pen.

Senator Ross was late for supper tonight, and when he took his place at our table, he refused a plate of food. He had just called at the White House, he told us, where he spoke at length with a servant. This afternoon Willie woke from his fever with a smile that lent hope to his mother's heart. But then, as the afternoon hours faded, Willie closed his weary eyes and died.

Silence fell upon us all. Although we had known that Willie was struggling with Death, none of us really believed he would lose the struggle. In the stillness of our sorrow, Senator Ross cleared his throat and in a sombre voice told us what he knew—in the first moments after Willie's death, Mrs. Lincoln stared at her son's white face as though she didn't recognize that he had died, but cruel realization soon struck and she threw back her head and screamed. Supposedly her screams were horrible to hear, like those of an animal caught in a trap. Then she grew wild with agony, and throwing herself onto the floor she lay prostrate with grief. Later, when Mr. Lincoln lifted the sheet covering his son's face, his own face became distorted and aged, and though anguish choked him, he whispered, "We loved him so."

Oh, Regina, we loved him so.

Monday, February 24

Today little Willie Lincoln was buried. I wanted to bare my head in respect and stand on the street as the funeral procession passed by, but Ma forbade me to leave the house, for a violent storm struck Washington—gales of wind blew off the roof of a neighbor's house, trees were uprooted and thrown across our street, and buildings collapsed and burst into flames.

This afternoon as I watched the grey rain and the slashes of white lightning and listened to the howling winds, I wondered if Nature was imitating the anguish of the Lincolns— the anguish of Mr. Lincoln as the tiny coffin was lowered into its cold grave and of Mrs. Lincoln as she mourned from her cold bed.

Oh, Regina, we must pray for our President—and for our Nation. Now that gentle Willie has been taken from our troubled world, there will be less laughter.

Friday, February 28

At supper tonight my sister was pushing her fork back and forth, her stew untasted. Ma asked Mary if she felt well, for indeed she looked pale and her eyes seemed larger than usual. In an unnatural voice my sister told us that she was suffering, not with sickness but with fear. Her eyes glittered with tears as she told of a disturbing rumor she had heard at work—that a Confederate army has camped outside the city of Washington.

Pa reached across the table and patted my sister's hand. "The rumor is true," he told her, which caused Mary's face to blanch even whiter, but he quickly added that we are in no danger because President Lincoln has ordered General McClellan to position his army so as to shield our city from invasion.

Mary was so pleased by Pa's good news that she devoured her stew and two pieces of rhubarb pie.

I must close now—my sister wishes to celebrate Pa's good news, so my family is gathering by the hearth to sing our favorite songs.

P.S.—I nearly forgot to tell you the best news of all. Pa told us that Mr. Lincoln has taken over as Commander of our Nation's armies until he can find a general more competent than McClellan! Pa is delighted.

Saturday, March 1

I must admit that I'm not surprised to hear that your heart and

Edward's have been pierced by Cupid's arrows—from all you've written about him in past letters, I knew that True Love had come to you both.

Regina, perhaps you and Edward should reveal your feelings for each other to your aunt and uncle. Then, when he asks permission to court you, they will be less hesitant to give their blessings.

This letter must be brief, for Pa and I are leaving for the Post Office in a moment so that I can mail you this letter and a parcel. This year my birthday gift to you is a sketch of a nearby river, the Potomac. Sometimes on windy days the river stinks of the raw sewage that is dumped into its depths. And yet there are long stretches of the river that are lovely, especially when sun rays sparkle on the waters like so many diamonds.

Dear friend, I wish you the happiest of birthdays.

Monday, March 24

Your letter brought tears to my eyes! How romantic to have received a marriage proposal on your birthday! Every girl should have a fifteenth birthday as memorable as yours! Oh, Regina—in two short years you will be Mrs. Edward Hamilton!

Thank you most kindly for asking me to be your Maiden-of-Honor. I accept most gladly! I agree that we should wear identical dresses, though only you should wear a veil of lace. My long hair will serve as my veil (my parents will never let me trim the mop I wear, even though the curls are thick and heavy).

My family shares my happiness. Mary dreams of meeting someone as remarkable as your Edward. My poor sister worries that she may become a spinster, for she has not received a single proposal and her sixteenth birthday is fast approaching. Ma and Pa are writing you a letter of congratulations. Ma is also writing to your aunt and uncle to thank them for their offer of lodging during the wedding week. Pa says we will travel by railroad, for the War will surely end within two years and trains will be safer and more affordable.

Dear friend, congratulations to you and Edward on your betrothal!

P.S.—I am pleased that you liked my sketch.

Thursday, March 27

Today Pa burst through the front door with exciting news from the War Department—finally, General McClellan's Army of the Potomac is marching off to battle. No, not really marching—Pa said all of the one hundred thousand soldiers are boarding boats on the Potomac River.

What a grand sight that must be, hundreds of boats overflowing with soldiers and horses and cannons! Although General McClellan's destination has been kept secret, Pa heard rumors that the general intends to sail his army to Virginia before marching up the Peninsula to invade Richmond.

Oh, Regina, if the rumor is true, Richmond will surely surrender and then the Confederacy must end their Rebellion. If so, this terrible War will end and my brother and Boudy and all the men of the grey and blue armies can return home.

Tuesday, May 6

I am sitting in my attic room watching the rain strike my windows. Rain has been falling for weeks. Pa said this same cold rain has been falling on Virginia, where the ground has become a sea of mud—a sea of thick, deep mud that slows the steps of our soldiers. Will they ever reach Richmond?

It sorrows me to think of those brave men struggling through the mud, marching and fighting and bleeding and dying in the mud. Eating and sleeping in the mud.

Will this Madness called War ever end?

I will close now, for the rains have darkened my room. I can no longer see to write, and I lack all desire to light my lamp.

Friday, July 11

I received your long letter about Edward enlisting in the Union Army. Try not to feel disheartened during his absence, Regina, and instead be proud of his desire to serve our Nation. He believes, as you do, in its Reunification, but because he is a man he can put those beliefs into action.

As you well know, I, too, believe in the Reunification of our Country, and I have not forgotten my vow to help Mr. Lincoln end this War. But how, Regina—how can I keep my vow?

My dear father is sitting downstairs staring at the cold ashes in the hearth. He has been sitting there for hours, for he is bitterly disappointed with General McClellan's failure to invade Richmond. Our army has begun its retreat back down the Peninsula—Pa told me that retreat is another word for defeat. Thousands of our soldiers died on that Peninsula, Regina. They died for nothing.

Pa said the Confederates have chosen a new leader for their armies, a regal officer named Robert E. Lee. Pa met General Lee when he still served in our Union's army—he remembers him as an honorable man who possesses both a brilliant mind and a fearless heart. Pa fears General Lee, for he could lead the Confederates to Victory.

I will close now and go downstairs and make my poor father a cup of lemon tea.

P.S.—Of course I will pray for your beloved Edward and for you, Regina.

Thursday, September 4

I am writing this letter in my attic room. Below my windows my neighbors are scurrying about like frenzied ants in a kicked anthill. I can see Mr. and Mrs. Browning loading furniture on an open wagon, for they are fleeing to Maine. I can see Mr. Grason boarding up his windows and his wife wringing her hands as she watches him.

Oh, Regina, my neighbors and the citizens of this city have been touched by panic, a wild sort of panic—panic that General Robert E. Lee will not be satisfied with last month's victory at Bull Run, panic that Lee will now invade Washington.

How is it possible that our army—our superior, larger army—could suffer a second defeat at Manassas, where Mary attended that wretched picnic luncheon? Understanding escapes me as I look down at the street and watch people rush by, their eyes widened by their fear of invasion. Some of that fear has trespassed into my house. For myself, I am somewhat calm until my imagination takes over and I imagine Rebel soldiers marching down my street. Mary has begged that we board a northbound train, but Pa refuses to flee and spends hours at the War Department learning what he can. Ma seems composed, but she has forbidden Mary and me to leave the house.

Earlier this morning, weary of our imprisonment, I pleaded for permission to sit on the front stoop. Ma finally relented on the promise that I not take a single step afar. I sat there for hours polishing and repolishing tarnished spoons while I listened to the conversations of those passing by.

Most interesting was a discussion between two soldiers who

had fought at the second battle of Bull Run. They happened to pause near my step to clean their smelly pipes—they must not have noticed me, for they swore rather much. The first soldier, a thinnish man with a crooked nose, spat at the road whenever the name of General John Pope was mentioned, clearly blaming him for their defeat at Bull Run. The other soldier, a shortish man with wiry hair, swore that the Confederates were victorious because they were led by brave and clever generals. One Confederate general whom they mentioned often has a rather peculiar first name: Stonewall. Stonewall Jackson.

As the soldiers walked away, one muttered something that made my heart stand still. He said that he could picture General Robert E. Lee tugging on his white beard and planning his Invasion of the North.

Regina, those words, "Invasion of the North," kept echoing in my ear until understanding came to me—I now know that Mary is wrong about escaping on a northbound train and that my neighbors are wrong to escape to Maine, for there is no safe haven in the North to escape to. We must wait quietly in our homes and hope that our army can protect us from invasion.

I'll close now, for I see Pa coming down the street and I am anxious to hear what he has learned at the War Department.

P.S.—Do you suppose that somewhere in the South lives a girl, a girl like you and me, who is fearful that Yankees will invade her city?

Thursday, September 18
Late last night Pa rushed in shouting great news—the Union won a battle at Antietam—General Lee's Invasion of the North has been halted by General McClellan's army!

This morning Ma made us a celebratory breakfast of salted bacon and biscuits with egg. While we ate, a neighbor stopped by with the latest news—the Confederate Army is retreating back across the Potomac River into Virginia.

Oh, Regina, the fear of Invasion has vanished from Washington like the smoke of a dying fire. Ma unlocked the doors and raised our windows, Mary rushed off to her job, and I returned to my wandering exploration of this vast city.

Everywhere I walked I saw the riot of celebration. On every street soldiers danced arm in arm, ladies and gentlemen waved small flags, and children threw colorful confetti. On every corner firecrackers exploded, voices sang out patriotic songs, and crowds cheered columns of troops.

I arrived home by suppertime and joined my family around the table for another meal of celebration. Ma made Pa's favorite dish, shepherd's meat pie, but he barely ate at all. Indeed, Pa spoke few words, which rather surprised me because yesterday night he couldn't contain his excitement. After supper he asked us to gather by the hearth, and as Pa spoke, I understood the reason for his sombre mood.

He told us about the battle that had been waged at Antietam. He told us much about the two giant armies that had fought on the banks of a creek, in cornfields and woods, across a churchyard and on roads. He told us that the battle had been bloody, for the soldiers fought savagely with rifles, fists, and sticks. And he told us that within hours thousands of men had been wounded, thousands had died, and thousands were now dying.

Regina, as Pa told us what he knew about Antietam I could see that he was sickened by what he had learned. I, too, lost all desire to celebrate.

I came up here to my room and looked through the windows at the bonfires of celebration. I thought of your betrothed, Edward, my beloved brother, Bob, and my dear friend, Boudy, and I wondered if they had fought at Antietam.

After a while I shut the drapes, for I couldn't bear to look upon the lights of victory.

Monday, September 22

Regina, you will never believe what happened at supper tonight! Senator Ross mentioned that he would miss a certain gentleman clerk at the Post Office because he handled congressional mail with great care (the clerk enlisted in our army). Then Senator Ross winked at me before telling my parents that he has suggested to the manager of the Post Office that I be hired in the clerk's place!

Pa said it was a capital idea, but Ma said no. I pleaded with Ma to change her mind, but it was Senator Ross's remark that I'd be safer in the Post Office than wandering the city's streets that won her over. Oh, Regina, Ma gave me permission to apply for the position on the morning of my fifteenth birthday.

Only two days to wait until Wednesday, and yet it seems so far away.

P.S.—I nearly forgot to tell you—Mary has a beau, a pleasant gentleman named Mr. Horace Sagely. They were fated to meet, for he owns a haberdashery on the floor above my sister's land office. Horace is tall and handsome and graciously kind. He served as a captain in our army until he lost his left eye at the Battle of Shiloh on the Tennessee River, and now he wears a black patch over his missing eye. Mary says the patch makes him look rather distinguished and mysterious.

Wednesday, September 24

My fifteenth birthday has come at last. I received some lovely gifts, though none of them quite matched the proposal you received on your fifteenth birthday. Thank you for the ribboned sachet, Regina. As always, your embroidery is lovely.

For my birthday supper Ma prepared my favorite dish, a delicious meat pie like the ones my Scottish grandmother often made.

Mary's beau, Horace Sagely, was invited to my celebration. He surprised me with a beautiful hat that has two large white roses on the brim (he asked Mary to choose any hat she wanted from his shop and Mary has such perfect fashion sense). I shall wear my rose hat everywhere.

Senator Ross attended my supper party, too. He kindly gave me a framed daguerreotype of our President taken by a gentleman named Mathew Brady. I have already hung Mr. Lincoln's likeness over my desk.

Pa gave me a copy of Mrs. Julia Ward Howe's patriotic poem, "Battle Hymn of the Republic" (set to the tune of "John Brown's Body"), and Mary gave me a painted tin of lilac-scented powder.

Oh, Regina, Ma gave me a most thoughtful gift, a dark blue dress of Scottish plaid with a collar of creamy velvet. Ma is so dear—she gave me the dress before breakfast this morning so I could wear it to my interview at the Post Office.

When I walked into the building I felt as though I had entered another world, for the Post Office is grand and elegant with marble floors and columns and ceilings that seem to reach upwards forever. A jovial gentleman named Mr. Donald Martin interviewed me (he reminded me of my father, for he was patient with my many questions). My penmanship and skills in

ciphering impressed him, and he shook my hand to welcome me into the postal service. I am now an official Postal Clerk for the United States government! On Monday of next week I begin my duties: sitting on a high stool and selling stamps through a window. And for simply sitting there selling those stamps I will be paid fifty dollars a month! Never again will Ma have to worry about finding money for Pa's medicines. I am so happy that I doubt my eyes will close all night.

P.S.—I may have discovered a way to keep my vow to help Mr. Lincoln end this War. Mr. Martin told me that because the Post Office has steam heat, the basement has been turned into a hospital for wounded soldiers. Surely my help would be appreciated.

Monday, November 17

This afternoon, after finishing my duties in the Post Office, I walked downstairs to the basement. At the door sat a plump lady, a Mrs. Wooten, whose smile lent me courage. I told her of my vow and asked if there was some way I could help in the hospital. Mrs. Wooten asked me my age and was surprised that I was fifteen years (she thought I was twelve because of my short height).

After asking me many questions, she discovered that I lacked training as a nurse, but I pleaded with her to overlook my inadequacies. She smiled and declared that she believed my intentions were sincere, then led me into another room. There she handed me a white apron to tie over my dress and pointed at straw baskets filled with rolled bandages. She said I could be of use to the surgeons by following them around and handing them bandages as needed. I picked up a basket and followed Mrs. Wooten towards another door even as I noticed a most dreadful smell, a putrid odor that I could not identify.

We entered yet another room where soldiers lay on cots or sat on chairs. Regina, I was not prepared for what I saw—soldiers of every age without legs or arms or hands or feet or eyes. I stared at their bandages, for they were dry with brown blood or wet with red blood. I listened to their moans of pain and pitiful pleas to be released from their suffering. And I smelled that foul odor again, which I then recognized as the stench of vomit, diarrhea, infected flesh, and death.

I am told that I fainted; I woke up in the outer room under the care of the kindly Mrs. Wooten. She asked me if I possessed the strength to face the misery in the rooms beyond, and I shook my head no. The very thought of nursing the wounded nauseated me.

Deeply ashamed of my weakness and with shaking legs I somehow managed to walk home. Ma met me at the door, and upon hearing my story she rushed me into a hot bath and then my bed.

Ma is so kind—she never criticized me for my weakness or reprimanded me for my boldness. Instead she told me of her doubts that I could ever nurse, for she said that I wear an artist's heart, a sensitive heart that feels others' actual pain.

Oh, Regina, I failed as a nurse, but I intend to keep my vow to help Mr. Lincoln end this War. But how shall I fulfill that vow?

I'll close now, for Ma is insisting that I put down my pen and rest.

Tuesday, December 16

Tonight, both Pa and Senator Ross were clearly troubled, so I begged Pa to tell what worries furrowed their brows. Pa sat in his rocker and Ma and Mary put down their sewing and joined me on the sofa. We sat, the three of us holding hands, while Senator Ross stood with his back to the hearth, for he seemed much too agitated to sit.

Pa told us that a battle ended yesterday—a terrible, bloody battle at a town in Virginia called Fredericksburg. Mary asked if our army had been victorious. We knew by the pain in Pa's eyes that it had not. Ma tightened her hand around mine as Senator Ross told of the slaughter of thousands of our Federal soldiers—oh, Regina, so many soldiers fell that the living were tripping over the bodies of the dead.

Then Senator Ross told of the thousands of Confederate soldiers who had also died at Fredericksburg, and as he spoke Ma's hand tightened painfully around my fingers—surely she thought of Bob, for it has been nearly a year since his letter arrived. We don't even know if he is still alive.

After they told us about the battle, Pa and Senator Ross grew quiet. Ma gestured at me and Mary to follow her into the kitchen. We prepared a fine meal, but the food seemed tasteless, for everyone's thoughts dwelt on the slaughter at Fredericksburg. I know with certainty that Ma thought about Bob, for her eyes wore a distant look, a most grievous look.

Thursday, December 18

On quiet days at the Post Office, when there are few customers and no one is speaking, you can hear the sounds of the hospital below. Although the sounds are often disquieting (I won't dwell on those, Regina), occasionally come more cheerful ones—laughter or the music of a squeaky piano.

Today I heard the most marvelous sound of all: I heard singing. A gentleman's voice, beautiful and clear and rich, floated upstairs through the heating pipes. All of us working at our windows and desks stared at one another, for the voice was that of an angel. Oh, Regina, I had never before heard such a heavenly voice! When the song ended none of us spoke a word, for we hoped to hear another song, but there was only silence. Disappointed, we returned to our work.

Throughout the morning hours I kept humming the lovely song—it was strangely familiar—and then with a sudden shock I knew why. The melody was the one that James Kilmar had whistled for me on the train—the song he had written for his mother.

During my luncheon hour I hurried downstairs to the basement, where I found Mrs. Wooten sitting at her desk. In a voice shaking with excitement, I told her about the boy soldier I had met on the train and asked if James Kilmar was the name of the singer who had sung so beautifully. It was he! Sadly, though, he had just left the building and she was not sure when he would return.

Mrs. Wooten and I spoke at length about James. She told me he had been brought to the Post Office hospital over a year ago, and after many months of care he had recovered enough to return home. Instead, he had refused to leave Washington, for he was determined to help with the wounded.

"How," I blurted out rather rudely, "when James has no hands?"

Mrs. Wooten's smile widened as she explained that James doesn't need hands for what he does. He possesses two rare gifts, the gift of storytelling and the gift of voice—gifts that allow soldiers in hospitals throughout the city to forget their suffering for a while.

Mrs. Wooten was unaware of James's decision not to contact his mother, and she agreed with me that Mrs. Kilmar should know that her son is here in Washington.

Upstairs I found a quiet desk where I wrote Mrs. Kilmar a long letter about everything—James's loss of his hands, his belief that the Peabody Conservatory would refuse his return as a student, his shame at facing her, and his generous work amongst the wounded. I ended the letter with an invitation to lodge with my family if she chose to come to Washington. Since I had no address for her, I simply marked the envelope with her name and the words "Annapolis, Maryland."

When I arrived home I told Ma about James and the letter I had written to his mother, and she hugged me fiercely, her eyes misting with tears. War is horrible, Regina, but especially so for mothers.

Wednesday, Christmas Eve
Never will I forget this Christmas! Early this evening while the goose was still roasting in the oven there came a knock at our door. A soldier about eighteen years of age stood on our step with his cap in his hand. He was as thin as a stick and unusually tall, even though he stooped a bit as if his shoulders couldn't bear life's burdens. In a quaint accent he introduced himself as Nathan Ennis from New Hampshire and while apologizing for interrupting our holiday he handed a letter to my father.

It was a white envelope—that is, the envelope had once been white—but it had been soiled and crumpled. Pa stared at the letter and then at Ma, and as if she understood Pa's expression she murmured, "Bob?" Pa, suddenly speechless, thrust the letter at her. Trembling, Ma tore open the envelope, and as she read Bob's letter out loud her eyes shone as bright as the Christmas Star.

Oh, Regina, my brother wrote that he is faring well; he made no mention of battle or deprivation. He begged for our understanding of his decision to support the Confederacy, and added his sincere wish that our Nation could be reunited in Peace. Bob closed his brief letter by writing that he loves us all and that he longs to see our faces.

In the excitement none of us noticed that the soldier had quietly left. Rushing outside, Pa and Senator Ross found Nathan standing on the corner and insisted that he share our Christmas goose.

Upon their return they met a woman alighting from a carriage. She asked Pa if he knew the house of Miss Vinnie Ream. I, standing in the shadow of the door, felt my heart flutter, for I knew at once that she was James's mother. (Indeed, Mrs. Kilmar and her son closely resemble each other in coloring and face.) I ran down the steps to welcome her to our home.

Senator Ross insisted on pouring out cups of Christmas punch, and while our guests warmed themselves by the hearth we heard their stories.

As Nathan drank from his cup I took a moment to study him discreetly. Black shadows hung under his large eyes, but they were beautiful eyes of green, and his face, though narrow, was pleasant. I listened carefully as he told us that he had met my brother last summer in a trench after a battle had ended. Both he and my brother were wounded. Neither suffered too seriously, but neither had the strength to climb out of the ditch. They lay there, each staring at the other, knowing that moments before the battle had ended they had tried to kill each other. All of a sudden they were laughing, loud fits of laughter born of their exhaustion. Then, their laughter spent, they told each other about their homes and families. They talked for hours until the medical wagons came and took them away—my brother to a Confederate hospital and Nathan to a Union one. Before they parted, my brother asked Nathan to carry a letter to my family if he happened to pass through Washington. The letter was dated June 1.

After Nathan had finished his account, Mrs. Kilmar told her own tale. She said she had received word over a year ago that her son had been wounded, but the message was brief and she didn't know the extent of James's wounds or if he had been hospitalized. As the days became weeks and the weeks became months she feared her son had died—until my letter arrived. It was a Christmas Wish fulfilled, Mrs. Kilmar said, smiling warmly at me.

Ma and I walked with Mrs. Kilmar to the basement of the Post Office, where we found Mrs. Wooten at her desk. After introductions were made, I asked if James happened to be working amongst the wounded in her hospital tonight. Mrs. Wooten smiled—we had come at a lucky moment. Taking Mrs. Kilmar's arm, she led her into the rooms beyond. They were gone a long time, and I began to fret that my letter had been a mistake, that James was displeased by his mother's visit.

All at once the very air quivered with the voice of an angel—James's voice, singing the song he had composed for his mother months ago while still a bugler in the army. His voice expressed such joy that Ma and I wept tears even as we smiled. After his voice had faded away, Mrs. Kilmar came through the door with her son, their own faces wet and smiling.

Supper was jolly, for the spirit of the Christmas Season encircled us all. Now the house is quiet at last. James and Nathan are asleep in the parlor and Mrs. Kilmar is comfortable in Mary's room. I am quite sure Ma and Pa are reading Bob's letter again and Senator Ross is asleep (we can hear his snores through the floorboards). Mary is sitting by my attic windows dreaming of her beau while I write this letter to you, my dear, dear friend.

Merry Christmas, Regina! And Merry Christmas to your aunt and uncle. I do so fervently hope that the New Year brings an end to this War.

1863

Thursday, January 1

My dear friend Regina,

Today Ma and I strolled arm in arm down Pennsylvania Avenue. Chilled by the air, we stopped for a cup of tea at a small hotel, and there, in the warmth of my mother's presence, I confessed my confusion about Boudy and John Rollin Ridge.

I told her of my disappointment that John has never written me, and avowed that I rarely think of him unless I am singing his poem. And I admitted that my thoughts linger on Boudy—too often I picture his dark eyes and wide smile and recall his laughter and witty words. And yet I am still angry with Boudy for choosing the Confederacy.

Ma smiled at my confession and said perhaps I think of Boudy because it is he whom I love, not John. She and Pa are certain that I would have married Boudy by my eighteenth birthday if we had stayed in Arkansas, she told me.

Her words should have startled me, but they did not, for my heart has known for some time what my lips would not speak— that I love Boudy with a passion that shall never be quenched. Oh, Regina, I doubt that Boudy and I will ever meet again, but he'll remain closeted in my heart forever.

My sweet mother spoke of others to distract my troubled heart. While we drank our tea we spoke about your coming marriage, about Mary's rejected beau (he didn't propose at Christmas, so Mary banished him), and about Pa's fragile health. In tears, Ma confided her worries about my brother, Bob, and I assured her that I pray for him every waking day.

When we left the tearoom we continued down Pennsylvania Avenue. We hadn't walked far when we heard the clatter of feet and saw a Negro gentleman running down the street waving a copy of the newspaper *The Evening Star*. Other men chased him, not to do harm, but wanting to read the newspaper he held. Catching him, they thrust him up on a box and called out, "Read, Reverend Turner, read," but he was gasping so horribly that he tossed the newspaper to another gentleman, who read, "President Lincoln has issued a proclamation that frees slaves in the states of rebellion … the Emancipation Proclamation."

His joyous words caused those listening, both white and colored, to clasp hands and dance wildly about. Amid the cheering and laughing and singing, a group of Negro children chanted, "Slavery chain done broke at last, broke at last, broke at last …"

From across the city, in the direction of the Navy Yard, we heard the roaring salute of cannons while all around us firecrackers popped and crackled. Ma and I rushed down the avenue to where a gathering of people paraded before the White House. As Ma and I looked on, there came a great cheer from the marchers. We turned to where they looked and saw Mr. Lincoln at a window, bowing to those celebrating his marvelous proclamation. Truly he is the Great Emancipator!

Happy New Year, Regina! Let's hope this year is especially happy and that the War ends quickly.

P.S.—Regina, however did my mother know that I love Boudy? Do mothers peek into the corners of their daughters' hearts?

Thursday, January 29

Last night Senator Ross was absent during supper, which surprised me, for he knew Ma would serve his favorite dish, Scottish stew. After we had eaten, my family retired to the parlor to sit by the fire. Pa and Ma sat together on our red sofa while Mary and I played chess on the hearth rug. The evening was lovely and peaceful; through the windows we could see the falling snow, but inside our parlor we were warm and happy.

When the hour grew late Senator Ross arrived home with such a solemn expression that we thought him ill. Ma brought him a plate of warm stew, but he ate very little. More than once he sighed loudly as though he had worries aplenty, and Pa asked what ailed him.

Sighing yet again, Senator Ross told us that he just learned that General Burnside has blundered as our new commander of the Army of the Potomac. He failed to reach Richmond by crossing the riverbed of the Rappahannock River. The riverbed wasn't empty—it was a trench of deep, deep mud. Our soldiers have become trapped up to their waists in the mud!

As though the news had aged him a hundred years, Senator Ross rose slowly from his chair and slipped into his coat. He intended to return to his office to learn further news, and Pa insisted on accompanying him. After they left, my sister asked Ma to help her upstairs with her sewing, and I was left alone in the parlor.

Outside the windows the night wind swirled the falling snow. I dimmed the lamps and lay down on the sofa, covering myself with the quilt. Warmly comfortable, I watched the fall of snow until my thoughts turned to the soldiers trapped under this same snowy sky in the muddy bed of the Rappahannock River. I thought of their cold misery without hearth or quilts to warm them, and the falling snow lost its beauty. After a while I closed my eyes.

I awoke to the sound of the front door closing softly. In the dark silence I heard Senator Ross and Pa speaking in lowered voices. Pa said, "Don't tell Lavinia or my daughters, especially Little Vin ... She is devoted to Mr. Lincoln—this treachery would sicken her."

Pa's words made me sit up. I swear I stopped breathing as I strained to hear more. Senator Ross said, "Vinnie will know all too soon, if McClellan takes over as our dictator ..."

I leapt to my feet and dashed out into the hallway, where I clutched at Pa's arm and demanded that he tell me the meaning of their words. He told me that some Republicans want Mr. Lincoln to resign as our President—indeed Mr. Lincoln is considering his own resignation, for he blames himself for every death of this War.

Sleep has escaped me this night. The sun will rise within the hour and soon we will know if Mr. Lincoln is still our President. Oh, Regina, if Willie had lived, Mr. Lincoln would possess the strength to throw off his despondency.

Friday, February 27

How joyous I felt when I learned that Mr. Lincoln will remain as our President. My joy melted away, though, when I read your last letter. Regina, I share your grief about Edward's capture and imprisonment at Castle Thunder. I know nothing of that place or of Petersburg, Virginia, but perhaps Senator Ross can make discreet inquiries. The moment he steps through the door I will ask him to learn all he can.

Take heart, Regina, and know that Edward is in my prayers.

Monday, March 16

I will be brief so that I can answer your question and mail this letter at once. No, dear friend, I am sorry to tell you that there is nothing more to be learned of Edward other than his continued imprisonment at Castle Thunder. However, Senator Ross did learn that Edward is faring as well as can be expected under the trying conditions that all Prisoners of War must endure.

Senator Ross has promised to write to you himself as soon as he learns more of your sweet Edward.

Friday, April 24

I am delighted to hear that Senator Ross's letter has lifted your spirits. Surely the War will end soon and then Edward will be home and you can plan your wedding day.

Thank you for asking about Pa's health. He is doing quite well, for we have extra money to buy him all the medicines he needs. Happily, I was able to provide that extra money, for I have been hired to sing in the choir of a local church. Can you imagine, Regina, how honored I felt when I discovered that I am the first woman to be hired to sing in the choir! When I arrived for practice I was surrounded by men and boys—Mary is rather envious, for she said I shall have my pick of beaux. I don't know about that, but I do know that it seems incredible that I am to be paid for doing what I love— imagine, three hundred dollars a year just for singing!

Music has entered my life in another way as well. Two weeks ago, I passed a Roman Catholic church and heard the sweet chords of harps. I tiptoed inside and sat in a darkened pew. Near the altar three nuns sat at exquisite harps made of polished rosewood with strings that shone like spun gold. One of them, an elderly nun, spied me sitting there, and in an Irish brogue she called out, "Are we being watched by an angel of God now?"

My cheeks burned with the embarrassment of discovery, and after apologizing for my rude intrusion I told them I had once taken lessons on the harp. As I turned to leave I could not help myself—I rushed up to them and confessed my love for the harp, and I begged that they accept me as their student. The

Irish nun smiled (her face was a wreath of wrinkles) and said they could not refuse the request of an "angel."

After a week of lessons I played and sang to the good sisters a beautiful song—the poem that John had written for me. The nuns were shocked to learn that the words of love had been written for me, and surprised that the poet was Cherokee. (The Irish nun, however, asked that I teach her John's song.)

Thursday, May 28

This afternoon my family received a letter from my brother that told of a battle in the Wilderness near Chancellorsville, Virginia. I had read about that battle earlier this month, but because I read the newspaper account with my Federal eyes I couldn't understand why our larger army had met defeat. Bob wrote about the battle as he saw it with his Confederate eyes— and now I understand.

Bob wrote that his commander, General Stonewall Jackson, noticed a weak spot in General Hooker's army: his unprotected right flank. Using the woods to shield his men from sight, Stonewall Jackson and thirty thousand soldiers stampeded up a path to attack that weak spot. Deer and rabbits fled in front of them as they burst into a Union campsite, yelling and shrieking to paralyze our Federals with fear.

Bob wrote that complete victory would have been theirs that day, but Union artillery and darkness caused them to pull back. Later that night Stonewall Jackson was riding back from a reconnaissance when he was accidentally shot by his own men. My brother accompanied the ambulance wagon to a hospital and waited nearby as General Jackson's arm was amputated. For days Bob watched over his beloved commander as he struggled with his infected wound and pneumonia. On the eighth day, my brother heard his general cry out in the delirium of fever before he lapsed into a quiet, peaceful voice and passed away.

Bob wrote that his grief for his commander was shared by his fellow soldiers and by General Robert E. Lee. Stonewall Jackson was much honored, Bob wrote, for his pious behavior, his courage under fire, and his brilliance as a military tactician. Bob told us General Jackson's principle of military strategy: "Always mystify, mislead, and surprise the enemy"—and that, dear Regina, is why the Union suffers such horrible defeats. As of yet, we have no generals who can mystify, mislead, and surprise our enemy.

Regina, is it possible that all the great generals of this War are fighting for the Confederacy?

Monday, June 1

Your sadness about Edward's ordeal as a prisoner is understandable, Regina, but perhaps I can offer you a distraction— why not come for a visit? Ma says you would be welcome for as long as you wish to stay, for the attic is spacious and there is always room at our table. Perhaps your guardians would consent to a visit if you told them that Washington is a city of marvelous wonders.

We could visit the "Red Castle," the Smithsonian Institution—a treasure house of the world's oddities and riches—and we could stroll through the institute's lovely gardens.

We could walk through the Capitol building—the dome is only half finished and there are blocks of marble waiting to be carved into statues, but you would be struck by the classic beauty that surrounds you there. (Mary refuses to look up at the half-completed dome, for she says it looms like a premonition of doom that our city will be under siege—Mary can be quite superstitious at times.)

Inside the Capitol I could show you such splendid statuary and paintings that your heart would flutter. I have memorized every curve, every line, and every shadow of each marble figure. Never do I tire of standing near, touching the cool, ice-smooth marble and imagining myself as the creator of such beauty. We could visit the wings of the Capitol as well—the Senate Chamber and the House of Representatives. Ma thinks the decor of brilliant reds and burnished gold is too bold and too lavish, but I drink in the color and richness.

While I work you could visit the Library of Congress— you could read every day from books that we once dreamt of reading, in elegant rooms that are as handsome as the books they house.

Regina, we could even visit the Lincolns' home—Mrs. Lincoln doesn't lock the front door of the White House until the hour grows late. I have discovered that it is possible to walk through the parlors on the first floor without being stopped by guards or servants. (Others must know this, for the newspapers report that knick-knacks have been stolen.)

The White House would remind you of a plantation down South. An iron fence with tall, graceful gates surrounds the front of the house while another iron fence encircles the rear. At the back there are wide kitchen gardens and fragrant greenhouses. Lovely lawns border the handsome house, and stone paths edged with flowers crisscross the green—we could walk on the northern pathways and hope to spy Mr. Lincoln and Tad playing on the lawns.

There is a smelly marsh at the end of President's Park, but we could press perfumed kerchiefs against our noses and cross over the poisonous water by way of high arching bridges. Once over, we would have to walk upon ground littered with bits of stonework and through grasses as high as our waists, but the walk would be worth all the bother, for the Mall must be seen. There you could see the memorial, a rectangular shaft of stone, that is being built in memory of President George Washington. Its construction cannot be finished until after this War ends, but once funds are again found, the shaft will loom high above the entire Mall like an arrow pointing towards the sun.

Regina, if you visit we could wear our finest dresses and carry lace parasols and walk on the northern end of Pennsylvania Avenue, where there are fashionable shops and ornate homes. If we could find gentlemen to invite us, we could dine at the Willard Hotel—that is where Washington Society meets for luncheons and afternoon teas. We would have to stay away from the southern end of the avenue, for it is impoverished and dotted with saloons and houses of ill repute. It is not that I feel above the poor (my family too has known poverty), but Ma has forbidden me to walk there because drunken soldiers frequent that end of the avenue.

Best of all, dear friend, we could stay up all night in my attic room talking about Edward and your coming marriage, about John and Boudy and Mr. Lincoln and everyone dear and precious to us. And perhaps, just perhaps, your loneliness would fade for a while.

P.S.—Regina, surely this War will end soon and you'll hear Edward's familiar step at your door.

Wednesday, July 8

Many months ago, during October of last year, Pa became ill at work and was carried home by some soldiers. The following day a messenger from a general named Ulysses S. Grant brought an urgent request that Pa complete the map he had been working on. The messenger stood guard at our front door while Pa, his legs wrapped in a warm blanket, finished marking a map of Vicksburg, Mississippi. Ma fretted while Pa worked, for she could see the perspiration of fever on his brow. Pa refused to rest, though, and after some time he laid down his pen, rolled up the map, and called for the messenger to deliver it to General Grant.

I had forgotten about that map until tonight, when Pa told my family that General Grant's army has taken the Confederate city of Vicksburg. Regina, the general's great victory has given our Union control of the Mississippi River—now the Confederacy has been split!

I asked Pa if the map he had drawn for General Grant had served in the victory; his answer was a small smile.

Tuesday, July 14

Last December I wrote you about Nathan Ennis, the soldier who delivered my brother's letter on Christmas Eve. Before Nathan left Washington, Ma made him promise to visit whenever he passed through our city. Tonight Nathan knocked at our door and we welcomed him to our table.

Nathan looked even thinner than he had at Christmas. Ma fretted that he was ill, but he said that the army's long marches steal the weight off his bones. He looked weary and we soon learned why. Nathan had just fought in the battle near Gettysburg, Pennsylvania, that stopped General Robert E. Lee's second invasion of the North.

Nathan said that on July 1 a Union spy reported that a column of Confederate troops was moving towards the small town of Gettysburg. The Confederates were searching for a shoe factory, for many marched barefoot and needed boots before autumn came. The Federals opened fire on the Confederates and thus that horrible battle began.

The fighting increased as the hot sun arched higher and higher in the sky, Nathan said, but by the time the sun had dropped from sight, the Union army had been pushed farther west to a place just south of Gettysburg, a place called Cemetery Ridge.

Nathan and his fellow soldiers were disheartened that night. As they sat around campfires eating brown beans, they tried not to notice who was missing, tried not to listen to the moaning of men who had suffered amputations of arms and legs, and tried not to worry that General Lee's army had won the first day of battle.

Nathan paused in telling his story and unbuttoned his shirt pocket. He withdrew a silver dollar with a dent in the center and handed it to my mother with a bashful smile. Ma examined the silver dollar before passing it around for the rest of us to see. Oh, Regina, Nathan carried that silver piece in his pocket throughout the first day of the battle—the coin stopped a bullet from piercing his heart! Now he carries it as his good-luck piece.

Nathan told us then about the second day of battle. As dawn broke, General Lee's army attacked like hungry wolves. They charged the Union's left flank at a place called Little Round Top, a hill that crested the southern end of Cemetery Ridge.

When that morning passed into afternoon the Confederates attacked again, but the Federals had moved to a peach orchard fronting Cemetery Ridge. The Confederates blasted their cannons, but the peach trees shielded the Federals and so the Confederates swarmed up Little Round Top. Nathan said that when he heard the afeared Rebel's Yell and saw the gleaming bayonets flashing in the sun, he thought General Lee would find complete victory at Gettysburg, but then, out of nowhere, Union cannons appeared on the stony hillside of Little Round Top—those cannons blasted furiously and the Confederates fell back.

Nathan paused. His eyes wore a distant look; I thought perhaps he was seeing the battle as clearly as if it were happening once again. We waited quietly until he continued his story, and in a voice that had deepened slightly he told of a small company of soldiers from Maine—perhaps four hundred men—who emptied their barrels before fixing their bayonets and charging downhill. Nathan is convinced that those men from Maine saved our entire Army of the Potomac.

At that very moment, Ma handed the silver dollar back to Nathan. He stared at the coin for a full minute and when he looked up his eyes rested on my mother's face. In a strangled voice he told her that as the battle waged on, he and a good friend fought side by side until his friend was struck in the neck by a barrage of bullets. The bullets severed his neck, and his head dropped at Nathan's feet.

Nathan's voice broke then, and his eyes glistened as my mother cradled him in her arms the way she had often cradled my brother. Pa glanced over at Mary and me and we hurried into the kitchen to put on the kettle. By the time of our return with tea and toast, Nathan looked more himself, and he continued his story while Ma poured out the tea.

On the third day of battle Nathan was woken by a burst of gunfire, for Confederate troops were assaulting Culp's Hill, a bit of land that rose at the curving top of the Union's line. The assault was fierce and bloody, but it failed. Then, for several hours, the battlefield was as quiet as a graveyard.

That faraway look glazed Nathan's eyes again when he confided that what he saw next sickened him. Across from him, west of Cemetery Ridge, was a wall of Confederate cannons that must have stretched for two miles. Nathan said he felt as though each and every cannon was pointed directly at him. He thought that by day's end he'd be dead.

Regina, the teacup rattled on Nathan's saucer as he spoke; it was obvious he was reliving that terrible time. He told us that the Confederates began blasting their cannons at noon, all of them firing at once. He described the noise as a million thunderclaps, deafening and terrifying to hear. For over an hour the cannon fire thundered, but luck held on the Union's side, for the gunners aimed a trifle too high and the shot fell largely at the rear of the Northern line.

Nathan said that all at once the cannons were silenced and in the eerie stillness he and his fellow soldiers stood up to see why the barrage had ended. Regina, Nathan's eyes widened when he told us what he saw—thousands and thousands of enemy soldiers, three ranks deep and two miles wide, advancing towards the Union line. Nathan said he just stood there as though in a trance and yet today he remembers each second of those horrifying minutes. He remembers seeing the flag of the Confederacy waving high above the soldiers' heads. He remembers hearing the thudding of drums and the blaring of bugles. He remembers the noble stance of Southern officers astride their horses, darting in and out of the ranks of men. And he remembers being blinded by the sunlight glinting off the barrels of rifles and the blades of swords and bayonets.

Nathan said that as the Confederates came closer and closer his stomach twisted into tight knots, but when he heard the order to open fire he shot his weapon. He swore to us that in spite of the noise of battle, he could hear the beating of his own heart, and with each beat hundreds of Confederates fell dead under the rain of Union bullets and shells. Within moments the entire left flank of the Confederate line had fallen. He learned respect for Southern bravery that day, Nathan told us.

The battle ended at last. Though he felt wearied to the point of exhaustion, Nathan could not sleep, for throughout the night he was haunted by memories of the line of cannons and the thud of drums and the fierce, proud faces of his enemy. Then, on the following morning, while General Lee's army slowly retreated back to Virginia, Nathan said he slept soundly even though rain poured down upon his head.

After his long visit Nathan took his hat, thanked Ma for her good supper, and walked slowly towards our door. He seemed hesitant to leave, as though there was one last thing he had to say. Turning to Ma he said, "I hope your son returns home to you at War's end." Tears welled up in Ma's eyes, and Pa quickly insisted that Nathan stay in our home for the time he has in Washington. Pa's invitation pleased Ma, for she dearly misses my brother. Having Nathan around for a few days somehow makes Bob seem closer.

Regina, Gettysburg is forever stained with the blood of soldiers. Our Nation will never forget the valiant men who fought there—both the courageous men of the North and the courageous men of the South.

Saturday, August 15

I received your copy of Edward's letter and agree with your reasoning that he is ill. Nothing else could explain his strange, rambling sentences. I showed the copy to Senator Ross and told him of your desperate appeal for his help to discover what he could of Edward's condition. I sorely wish I could conceal what he learned through his congressional office, for I despise bearing bad news, but I will honor your plea for truthfulness.

Regina, a deadly epidemic of measles has swept through Castle Thunder. Both Union prisoners and Confederate guards have fallen prey to the disease; many have died, while many more are expected to die. Dear friend, Edward is listed amongst the ill.

Take heart, Regina, for Senator Ross has arranged for a minister to visit your Edward and bring him spiritual comfort, food, and medicine. I will write you as soon as there is further word. Until then, dear friend, try to find comfort in your prayers.

Friday, August 21

This is the most difficult letter I have ever written, for each word is torn from my heart. If I could hide the truth from you, I would—but I cannot. Dear friend, your beloved Edward died early yesterday morning.

You have a right to know the complete truth, and so I will tell you everything I know.

Senator Ross's friend, the Reverend Josiah Baxter, was permitted inside Castle Thunder to visit Edward. Reverend Baxter said that the stink of tobacco, which still hung in the air from the prison's former days as a tobacco warehouse, choked him, for there were no open windows. All around him prisoners pleaded for water. As he poured water into their cupped hands he asked each man if he was Edward Hamilton. One soldier, grateful for a cooling sip of water in the oppressive heat, pointed to another soldier lying in a dark corner—your beloved Edward.

The good reverend took off his coat, bunched it into a crude pillow, and placed it under Edward's head to give him some comfort. He offered water, but Edward refused it with his eyes and Reverend Baxter knew at once that Edward was dying. Bending closer the reverend said, "I come on behalf of your betrothed, Regina."

At the mention of your sweet name, Edward moved his parched lips to speak but could not, and so the minister wet Edward's mouth with water. Again he struggled to speak. Finally, in a dry, hoarse voice, he whispered, "Regina is my joy." Then, even as his eyes closed in eternal sleep, Edward smiled—Reverend Baxter said that his smile transformed his sickly face into a face of tranquility.

Regina, if I knew the words that could lighten your heavy heart I would write them over and over again—but I fear that no such words exist.

Tuesday, September 1

You were overgenerous in your praise of my sketch—I merely read your old letters about Edward and used your words as a guide to paint his portrait.

My family and I are keenly disappointed that you will not visit us after all. Ma understands your aunt's concern about the perils of train journeys—even here in Washington we have heard stories about those villainous brothers Frank and Jesse James.

Perhaps, Regina, when this War finally ends, train travel will be safe again and we will visit each other.

P.S.—I wish I had met your sweet Edward, but somehow I

came to know him and love him through your letters.

Thursday, September 17

For the past several months I have been hiding a secret deep in my heart. Today I revealed that secret for the first time.

Do you recall that dream I once wrote you about—the dream in which the Indian children melted under the rain and, saddened, I took colored rocks and shaped statues of them? Over the past years that same dream has visited my sleep until I finally understand its meaning—that I must take rocks of marble and sculpt statues of those I love. I intend to become a sculptress!

Until today I kept my secret sealed within my heart, for Ma and Pa have always struggled to find money for medicine and food. I knew that they couldn't afford to provide the lessons I would need or buy the clay and tools sculptors must use. All that has changed, and I shall tell you why.

Often, when time allows, I walk through the Capitol to look at the statuary. In the Rotunda I have a special spot where I stand, and unobserved I study the statues and touch the cool, smooth marble. Today, someone did observe my reflective study, for a gentleman asked, "Aren't you Miss Vinnie Ream?"

Startled, I turned around and recognized at once the kindly face of Congressman James Rollins of Missouri. I was flattered that he remembered me, for we had only met that one time at Christian College when he visited with your uncle, and yet he clearly remembered my sketches and insisted that my artwork had revealed talent. He told me that he noticed me today because I appeared to be in a trance while staring at a statue.

I don't know what possessed me, Regina, but I confessed to him my dream of becoming a sculptress. He regarded my declaration as serious and we spent the next hour speaking of different sculptors and their works. While we spoke we walked around the Rotunda pausing before each statue. In front of Mr. Horatio Greenough's statue of George Washington I told the congressman that I found the piece offensive. Oh, Regina, the statue would offend you, too, for Mr. Washington is missing his clothes and he resembles the Greeks' mythological god Zeus! Congressman Rollins confided that the statue offends many Washingtonians and there is talk of moving the piece out of the Rotunda.

We spoke, too, of other statues around the city. We both agreed that Mr. Clark Mills's equestrian statue of Andrew Jackson in Lafayette Square is magnificent. I admitted my obsession with the statue and told of my frustration to determine how Mr. Mills could sculpt the horse with its legs rearing up in the air.

After a while we walked outside and stood looking up at the unfinished dome of the Capitol building. When I happened to mention my impatience to see the statue that Mr. Mills is casting for the dome's top, Congressman Rollins invited me to meet the famous sculptor—it seems, dear friend, that he and Mr. Mills are old friends! I accepted the congressman's kind invitation at once. We went back into the Capitol to the wing that houses the studio of Mr. Clark Mills.

The studio was a wondrous place. The room was filled with bags of dry plaster and boxes of shredded rags. Along three walls were narrow tables crowded with oddly shaped tools, misshapen wire, and buckets of dirty water. Dust floated through the stale air, which smelled of coffee and tobacco and wet clay. The floor was covered with bits of smashed plaster, and the corners were piled with torn paper and fragrant wood shavings.

Mr. Mills received us most graciously, but upon learning of

my desire to sculpt he tore off a large piece of clay, tossed it at me, and said, "Do a portrait of me."

I barely caught the clay, but I sat down at once and began to shape Mr. Mills's rather ordinary face. My fingers pushed and shaped and prodded the clay. The result, though crude, must have interested him, for he asked me to try a portrait of a more familiar subject. I thought immediately of Boudy's handsome face, but I am still vexed by him, so I chose to do a portrait of a childhood friend, a Wisconsin Indian.

I helped myself to more of the clay, and for the better half of an hour I pressed and prodded and shaped the moist stuff. I actually forgot that I had an audience as the clay took on a life of its own under my fingers. You see, Regina, at that very moment my dream was being realized—just as I had once dreamt of shaping rocks into Indian children, I was shaping clay into a familiar face with noble features and a feathered headdress.

Mr. Mills watched my work with growing interest, twice offering suggestions, and after I had finished he said, "Miss Ream, you will become a sculptress." He offered me then a most wonderful gift—in exchange for cleaning his studio and preparing his clay, I will be given lessons!

Regina, when I arrived home I burst into the parlor to tell Ma and Pa of my adventure. They had company, a rather nosy neighbor named Mrs. Pennyton. Ma noticed my soiled dress (more than once I had dropped wet clay on my lap), and as I explained my dress my excitement escaped me—I told of my meeting with Mr. Mills and his invitation to me to study in his studio.

Mrs. Pennyton's eyebrows shot up into little points. In a rather piercing voice she asked if I intended to study anatomy in order to sculpt. Her blunt question caused Ma's cheeks to flame red. Oh, Regina, how I regretted telling my news in front of Mrs. Pennyton, for Ma's hands trembled when that dreadful woman repeated her sharp question: would I study anatomy in order to sculpt?

I nodded yes, and with a gasp Mrs. Pennyton put down her teacup and hurried through the door without bidding us farewell.

Squeezing Ma's cold hands I told her and Pa about my recurring dream and how I finally realized its meaning. My mother was not impressed by my heartfelt declaration. She forbade me to sculpt, for she said that the study of anatomy would lead to disgrace and frighten away gentleman suitors.

Pa laughed and reminded Ma that there are sculptresses with fine reputations in spite of their study of anatomy, and some of them had married well. And so, dear friend, with Pa's good help, Ma finally relented. Upon my sixteenth birthday I will be allowed to study under Mr. Mills! Oh, Regina, my birthday isn't for an entire week. How slowly time is passing, each second lasting an eternity.

Thursday, September 24

Finally my sixteenth birthday has come! This afternoon I arrived at Mr. Mills's studio dressed in my Scottish gingham and my pretty rose hat. When I walked through his door my heart nearly burst with joy, for I felt as though I had walked into my dream.

Mr. Mills treated me with the utmost respect. Although two distinguished visitors—a handsome lady who wished her portrait done and a congressman wishing to discuss the casting of Thomas Crawford's statue, "Armed Freedom," that will top the Capitol's dome—awaited him, he led me over to a table for my first lesson.

The table had a curious design. Three sides were edged with a raised border and the back of the table was edged with a high board; a thin wire was strung taut from the front edge of the table to the top of the backboard.

Mr. Mills handed me a lump of soft, sticky clay and explained that clay is nothing more than water mixed with substances from the earth. He told me to hold the clay up, and when I did as he asked, it sagged in my hands. Mr. Mills explained that clay must be prepared to the right consistency for sculpting—it cannot sag, be too sticky to shape, or be too soft or too hard. The sculptor must mix the soft, sticky clay with a substance called grog. Grog is made from clay that has already been fired (baked in an oven until it hardens) and broken into pieces small enough to pass through a wire screen.

Today's lesson was to mix a tub of perfect clay. Under Mr. Mills's watchful eye, I first weighed some soft, sticky clay so as to calculate the amount of grog I had to add (only one quarter of the final clay mixture can be grog). I then spread the soft clay on the table until it measured one inch thick, and then, using my thumbs, I pressed dozens of dents into the clay. Next, I dampened the correct amount of grog and spread it over the soft clay before kneading the mixture with my fingers (much as bread dough is kneaded). Then I rolled up the mixture and kneaded it again with the heels of my hands until the clay took on a spherical shape. I pushed and kneaded the clay until it resembled a thick log, and then I pushed the clay against the wire strung across the table to cut the mixture in half.

The first half I threw down on the table and then, as Mr. Mills instructed, I threw the other half on top of the first piece. Again and again I kneaded and pushed and cut and threw down the pieces until Mr. Mills was satisfied with the consistency of the mixture. He said that with daily practice I should be able to prepare twenty pounds of grogged clay within minutes!

When the clay was perfect for sculpting, Mr. Mills instructed me to work with it as I wished. So, while he spoke with his visitors, I spent another hour pushing and twisting and pressing the clay with my fingers.

Oh, Regina, the clay I created was beautiful. Its appearance was different from ordinary clay, for the broken bits of grog lent sparkle to the mixture. The clay felt rather porous, bending and moving under my fingers as though it understood my intention and desired to please my creative touch.

When I arrived home Ma asked a thousand and one questions, for she is still worried about the morality of my lessons. Pa assured Ma that Mr. Mills is a reputable instructor, but she wasn't satisfied until I described him as the gentleman he is. I took care to hide my weariness from Ma, although my arms ached so horribly that it even pained me to lift my fork while I ate.

My birthday supper was a happy occasion. Ma had made a pie of pork and vegetables and for dessert we ate cherry cake. My family's gifts were especially thoughtful: Ma had sewn me a large checked apron to wear while sculpting, Mary had bought me a white gypsy scarf to tie back my hair while I sculpt, and Pa gave me a book about famous American sculptures.

Senator Ross wasn't home for my party, but he sent a box of foil-wrapped chocolates. (Mary loves sweets, so she has nearly emptied the tin.) All of us miss him. He visits his wife and children—who, as you know, live in Kansas—whenever possible. He will return to Washington in a fortnight.

How kind of you, Regina, to always remember my birthday. Whenever did you find the time from your studies to knit such a lovely shawl? I shall wear it proudly. Dear friend, many thanks.

Saturday, October 17
I have changed my hours at the Post Office so that I now work half days. And yet much activity crowds my days and spills over into my nights.

Each day, after working mornings at the Post Office, I prepare Pa's noon meal and we eat together by the hearth (how I delight in my hour with Pa!). Afterwards I hurry to Mr. Mills's studio in the Capitol building for an afternoon of cleaning floors, grogging clay, and learning the craft he has perfected. Before supper I stop by the Catholic church for a harp lesson with the good nuns, or at my neighborhood church for choir practice.

Recently, one other activity claimed much of my time. My manager at work, Mr. Donald Martin, asked me to take charge of the Post Office's part in Washington's Sanitary Fair. Large posters were printed giving my name and address and stating that I would accept contributions of stationery for our soldiers. So many boxes of stationery were dropped at my house that three horse-drawn carts were needed to carry them away! I am happy to report, Regina, that with the entire city taking part the fair was an enormous success—we raised over two thousand dollars for our good soldiers. Can you imagine how many shoes and blankets and coats the money will provide?

Tonight, all of us who had volunteered for the Sanitary Fair were invited to attend a benefit performance of William Shakespeare's play *Macbeth*. The beautiful actress Miss Charlotte Cushman played Lady Macbeth so wickedly and Mr. James Wallack was striking as her hapless husband.

Regina, Mr. and Mrs. Lincoln and their little boy, Tad, were in attendance. They shared a lower stage box, and because they sat directly to my right I could observe Mr. Lincoln whenever I liked. He once wrote that "nothing equals *Macbeth*," and indeed his eyes were fixed on the stage despite the fact that his son was restless, even climbing onto Mr. Lincoln's back. After the curtain had dropped for the final time, Miss Cushman was escorted on stage to receive a glorious bouquet, and she curtsied gracefully to Mr. Lincoln and his family and then to us, her audience.

The evening was enchanting. Indeed, I was frocked like a princess in a lovely gown of the softest rose, my hair was pinned up with ribboned combs, and my escort was a handsome gentleman who sings with me in the choir. All the magic of a fairy-tale romance was there, but my heart cast off the bewitchment of love. For you see, dear friend, each time I glanced over at my escort I wished Boudy were sitting there in his place. Oh, Regina, will I ever see Boudy again?

Friday, November 20

Late last night, Pa and I drove Senator Ross's carriage to the station to meet his train from Pennsylvania—he had accompanied President Lincoln to Gettysburg for the dedication of our National Cemetery. We waited on that windy platform for ever so long until the train pulled in, after the midnight hour. As the passengers alighted, I searched their faces, hoping to glimpse Mr. Lincoln—when I saw him, Regina, my heart crumbled into dust, for his face wore an expression of unfathomable sorrow.

Pa spotted Senator Ross at the far end of the train, and so, forcing myself to look away from Mr. Lincoln's sad face, I followed Pa down the platform.

Although the night was half gone by the time we arrived

home, my parents urged Senator Ross to tell of the day's affair at Gettysburg. We sat, my parents, my sister, and I, by the hearth with cups of sweetened tea and listened attentively.

Senator Ross told us that the ceremony started with a procession led by President Lincoln. He rode on a beautiful chestnut horse that supposedly was the largest horse in the Cumberland Valley, but Mr. Lincoln's towering stature seemed to shrink the animal's size. Behind Mr. Lincoln followed representatives of the government, military, and navy, troops of marching men, governors, and congressmen, and proud citizens of Pennsylvania.

From his own saddle Senator Ross noticed that Mr. Lincoln started the parade in regal form, for he sat his horse elegantly with the reins held high in his white gloved hands, his shoulders squared and his silk hat rising up over the heads of all others. But then, as the parade continued past makeshift hospitals where wounded soldiers peered from open windows and flags hung at half-mast, the President's shoulders rounded and his head bowed down with obvious despair. Senator Ross was certain, Regina, that the President's thoughts dwelt on the slaughter that took place there only four months earlier.

When the senator entered the cemetery, he was astonished to see the many thousands who had gathered to honor our country's dead. He took his seat on the platform near Mr. Lincoln and listened while a band played patriotic music for nearly an hour because the principal speaker, that famous orator Mr. Edward Everett, was late.

Mr. Everett arrived around noon. He began his speech in a powerful voice that rang out over the thousands listening or wandering about the fields. As he spoke, he flung back his white hair and used his hands theatrically like a great actor. Mr.

Everett spoke for nearly two hours! Regina, could you imagine standing there on that field for hours? Even Senator Ross admitted that after the first hour his thoughts drifted as he looked beyond the audience at the stubble of razed wheat fields, the skeletal branches of barren peach orchards, and the grassy slopes that reached afar to the blue-hazed mountains of the Cumberland.

And he said that as he looked out over that peaceful valley he thought of the bloody battle that had raged there last summer, for the fields, though green again under the November sky, still bore the stain of War. He imagined the soldiers, clad in grey and blue, rushing across the fields with rifles and bayonets. He imagined the smoke and the noise of battle that clouded the air for three long days. And he imagined the grasses drenched by blood until the green fields changed into fields of red.

Senator Ross said he was aroused from his sombre thoughts by the sound of applause as Mr. Everett's speech ended. An ode was then sung by a glee club from Baltimore. While they performed, Senator Ross watched Mr. Lincoln. He had put on his steel-bowed glasses and taken two papers from his coat, which he glanced over before returning them to his pocket. Then, the ode over and his name announced, President Lincoln took his place before the quieted audience. Holding the papers—his speech—in one hand, he spoke in a slow voice pitched high and clear and strong enough to carry out over the thousands standing before him.

At that point in the senator's story, he took from his own pocket a long sheet of paper—a copy of Mr. Lincoln's Gettysburg Address. Handing the paper to me, Senator Ross bade me read Mr. Lincoln's speech to my parents and sister.

I read aloud, how I don't know, for as I read Mr. Lincoln's words I felt choked with pride. I read:

> *Four score and seven years ago our Fathers brought forth on this Continent a new Nation, conceived in Liberty and dedicated to the proposition that all men are created Equal.*

Oh, Regina, in his opening words President Lincoln declared his belief that all men, white and colored, are born equal and thus deserve equal freedom! And then, dear friend, Mr. Lincoln reminded us that freedom is precious and dear, which is why our men willingly sacrifice their lives in this great struggle for freedom—this struggle we call War. President Lincoln continued:

> *Now we are engaged in a great Civil War, testing whether that Nation or any Nation so conceived and so dedicated can long endure. We are met on a great battlefield of that war. We have come to dedicate a portion of that field as a final resting-place for those who here gave their lives that that Nation might live. It is altogether fitting and proper that we should do this.*
>
> *But in a larger sense, we can not dedicate—we can not consecrate—we can not hallow—this ground. The brave men, living and dead, who struggled here have consecrated it far above our poor power to add or detract. The world will little note, nor long remember, what we say here, but it can never forget what they did here. It is for us the living, rather, to be dedicated here to the unfinished work which they who fought here have thus far so nobly advanced. It is rather for us to be here dedicated to the great task remaining before*

us—that from these honored dead we take increased devotion to that cause for which they gave the last full measure of devotion—that we here highly resolve that these dead shall not have died in vain—that this Nation, under God, shall have a new birth of freedom—and that government of the people, by the people, for the people, shall not perish from the earth.

After I had finished reading Mr. Lincoln's speech, the only sound in the parlor was the crackling of the hearth's fire. For a minute no one spoke, no one moved. Then in a low voice Pa said, "Mr. Lincoln has defined democracy."

Oh, Regina, truly Mr. Lincoln spoke from his heart. Surely every heart will hear and understand his simple words.

I asked Senator Ross what had happened after Mr. Lincoln finished his speech, and he told us that the audience stood silent, uncertain if Mr. Lincoln had finished since he had spoken for only two short minutes. But when Mr. Lincoln folded the two papers and returned to his seat, the audience applauded, though timidly, perhaps still puzzled by the brevity of his remarks, and soon the speakers and audience ambled from the cemetery towards horses and carriages.

Senator Ross told us that he returned to the cemetery later that night as the moon began its climb over the blue mountains. Alone in the silence of the graveyard he felt surrounded by the spirits of the fallen soldiers, both Union and Confederate. He understood then Mr. Lincoln's words that the ground he walked on had been hallowed by the soldiers' deaths. He understood, too, that they had sacrificed themselves for a principle worth dying for: Freedom.

And he told us that as he turned to leave he spied an aged

woman, dressed in black, walking between the white stones that marked the soldiers' graves. She held a lantern high and looked about as though searching for something of great value. Senator Ross offered assistance, and she explained that she sought her grandson's grave. As there was yet time before his train left, Senator Ross joined her search.

Evidently, Regina, the cemetery is not yet completed. Wherever the senator and the lady walked they had to step around the rotting carcasses of horses that had fallen during the battle (indeed, the dead horses are being blamed for infecting the children of Gettysburg with illnesses). For a full hour they searched under the moon's light until they came again to the row of graves marked for the "Unidentified" soldiers. There, the woman paused and said, "This is where my grandson lies."

Regina, every soldier who died in that battle has left behind grieving parents and grandparents like that poor, elderly woman. Mr. Lincoln understands such grief, for he himself has lost a beloved child. I truly believe he has taken on their sorrow as his own and their sorrow has scarred his gentle face with sadness.

Thursday, Christmas Eve

Ma and Pa are downstairs by the hearth reading my brother's most recent letter for the hundredth time. Bob wrote that he is troubled by the Confederate's recent defeats, but otherwise he is well in health and spirit.

Nathan Ennis sent my family a Christmas letter too. He kindly thanked Ma for her hospitality when last he was in town. Did I ever mention that Nathan's own mother died when he was a babe? He has grown fond of my mother and she speaks fondly of him. Pa says that her heart is a compassionate heart, for she mothers every motherless child.

Mary is sitting before my looking glass buffing her finger-nails. Her beau is dining with us on Christmas Day and she believes he intends to propose.

Earlier today I walked to the basement hospital under the Post Office, where I paused ever so long outside the door until I mustered the courage to knock. As I had hoped, Mrs. Wooten sat at her desk. In a rush of words I begged her to give me another chance to prove myself a nurse. Mrs. Wooten put up her hands to stop my pleading and asked me one question, "Is it true you sing in a choir?" When I nodded, a smile brightened her face.

Regina, Mrs. Wooten then told me marvelous news: James Kilmar's mother was able to arrange for his return to the Peabody Conservatory of Music! Although Mrs. Wooten shared my delight in James's good fortune, she was dismayed by his sudden absence, for the wounded would be without music for Christmas. She asked me to dismiss the notion of nursing and instead consider singing for the patients—she confided her belief that music heals the wounded as much as clean bandages. Oh, Regina, I hugged that blessed lady and together we entered the rooms beyond the door.

I would be a liar if I told you that the sight of those poor, mangled soldiers did not upset me—a liar if I told you that the smell of blood and vomit and infection did not nauseate me— a liar if I told you that all those pain-narrowed eyes staring at me didn't cause me to stumble as I walked. But I can tell you quite truthfully that never did I feel more like singing.

After an hour or so, during which I sang every Christmas carol I knew, I saw Mrs. Wooten beckon to me, and as I passed by the cots I took the soldiers' outstretched hands and mur-mured, "God bless you" or "Merry Christmas" or "God keep you." In truth, I no longer noticed their bandages or smelled foul odors; I only noticed the gratitude in their eyes.

At last, Regina, I have found a way to keep my vow to help Mr. Lincoln! I shall help his soldiers—not by collecting stationery or donating food, but by bringing them the gift of music that allows them for a moment to forget their misery.

I must close now, for Mary and I must change our dresses. We are going to the midnight service at church, and as a member of the choir I must arrive early.

Merry Christmas, Regina, to you and your dear aunt and uncle.

1864

1 8 6 4

Wednesday, February 3

My dear friend Regina,

For several weeks I have been learning how to use the different sculpting tools in Mr. Mills's studio. I feel rather clumsy at times, but with use they will, I hope, feel like a natural part of my hand.

Regina, a sculptor's tools are simple tools with simple purposes—they are used either for cutting off clay or for pressing on bits of clay. When I have to cut off large pieces of clay I use a fettling knife because it has a large blade. When I cut off small bits of clay or need to cut sharply into the clay I use an assortment of tools with wire loops at either end. And when I add texture to the clay (such as in the shaping of hair or eyebrows) I use tools with oddly shaped blades that are rounded or flat or sharp.

Last week, I was cutting off a thick wedge of clay when the fettling knife slipped and gashed my thumb. Blood ran over the grey clay and dripped onto my shoe, but I continued cutting off the wedge until I was satisfied. Then I pressed my thumb against my apron until the lesson had ended, for I didn't want Mr. Mills to note my carelessness.

At home, I had to hide my cut thumb from Ma, and so I feigned a headache and asked to be excused from supper. Up in my attic I tied a rag tightly around my wound, for it still bled freely.

The next morning I was awoken by a throbbing in my hand, for my thumb was red and much swollen with infection. My first thought was that my thumb would have to be amputated. I was horrified, for a sculptor needs the full use of both hands. I had no choice, Regina, but to confess my injury to Ma.

Angry that I had deceived her, Ma led me into the kitchen

and washed my hand with a bar of lye soap. She then removed a small wooden box from the back corner of her cupboard. Inside the box was a block of yellow cheese covered with a slimy green skin that stunk worse than an angry skunk.

I held my nose as Ma took a sharp knife and sliced off a chunk of the green stuff, and when she ordered me to eat it, I refused. Ma, with her usual patience, explained that whenever her clan in Scotland suffered infections, they ate the green slime that grew on old cheese and bread, and mysteriously their sores healed. And so, after quick consideration of my choices, I closed my eyes and ate the awful stuff.

Twice a day for over a week I had to eat a piece of that green slime, but by the tenth day the redness and soreness had disappeared from my thumb.

From now on I shall use the sculpting tools with greater care, for the very thought of that wooden box of slimy cheese sickens me.

Tuesday, March 8

Today, as has been my custom of late, I stopped by the hospital under the Post Office. When I first arrived I wrote letters for those soldiers unable to write home, and then I played my guitar and sang for the men.

I had sung only the opening stanzas of my first song, a long ballad, when I noticed excited movements by the patients and then unusual silence. I feared that some poor soul had just died, but then I saw the cause of their silence.

Behind me, mere feet away, stood a soldier, a private dressed in a faded blue uniform with worn, muddied boots. He was rather short, with rounded, stooped shoulders, and his appearance was small of bone. His face appeared scarred by hard times, but his countenance bespoke calmness. Though I noted the unevenness of his tattered nut-brown beard, I noted too that his blue eyes shone with a clearness rarely seen. He was bending over one of our dying soldiers, his thin hand resting on the man's shoulder with a gentle touch as though he were the boy's father.

Regina, I stared at that soldier in utter amazement, for despite his private's uniform, he was, in fact, a general—General Ulysses S. Grant—our Nation's greatest hope for Victory.

My amazement choked me and I lost my voice. General Grant glanced my way and said, "Please, miss, don't allow my intrusion to interrupt your song—these men desperately need some pleasure in their lives. From what I have just heard, your voice provides that."

Oh, Regina, I sang then without hesitation, for General Grant's words swelled my heart with joy. I sang and I sang and I sang long after General Grant had ended his visit. And while I sang I vowed to myself that I would sing to our wounded soldiers every day of this dreadful War.

I hurried home and burst into the house to tell my family about my meeting with General Grant. I had to wait to tell Mary, however, for she had just driven off in the carriage of her beau, Mr. Godfrey Anderson.

An hour later I heard the sounds of a departing carriage and Mary's step at the door. When my sister came into the parlor I thought how beautiful she looked. She wore a lemon-colored gown and her golden hair was twisted into a crown of curls around her heart-shaped face. Mary sat beside Pa on the sofa, and before I could tell her my news of General Grant, she surprised us with news of her own. Mary had just met General Grant! I laughed out loud and quickly told Mary of my own meeting with the general and then begged her to tell us of her meeting.

Mary told us that Mr. Anderson drove her to the Willard Hotel for supper, where they sat at an elegant, candle-lit table near a window. The evening should have been perfect, but Mary was uncertain if she cared for Mr. Anderson. From the first moment that she had stepped into his carriage he had spoken continuously about himself—his education, his wealth, his accomplishments, his honors, and so on and on. Mary said that as she sat there listening to his bragging she became vexed, disturbed by the notion that perhaps all successful men speak of themselves incessantly.

At that moment, Mary told us, a loud cheer rose up around her and she looked towards the open door. General Ulysses S. Grant stood there as though frozen to the floor with a thick cigar clamped between his teeth. He looked embarrassed as gentlemen and ladies pounded their tables with forks and fists, waved napkins like small flags, and whistled and clapped and cheered for him.

Mary said that General Grant sat down at the table beside hers, from where she could steal glances at him and overhear snatches of conversation. Sitting with him was a boy of perhaps fourteen years whom he addressed as Fred; Mary soon realized that Fred was the general's son. The cheering continued, and after a while General Grant stood up, wiped his mouth with his napkin, and bowed to the diners—he was clearly embarrassed and perhaps a trifle annoyed. Finally the company quieted, which allowed the general and his son peace in which to enjoy their meal.

At that moment Mary's vexation ended. Near her sat a general of great importance and popularity, and yet he sat modestly, quietly, wishing for none of the turmoil he caused by his mere presence. Mary took a long, hard look at the conceited Mr. Anderson and bade him drive her home at once. Telling the story now, my sister turned to Ma and made her promise to refuse Mr. Anderson's card if he should call again.

Later, as the fire in the hearth flickered and faded away, Senator Ross arrived home with news of his own—he, too, has met General Grant!

Senator Ross said he stopped by the White House tonight for the President's public reception. The senator was speaking to Mrs. Lincoln when it was announced that General Ulysses S. Grant was at the door, asking for President Lincoln. The citizens who were there to meet our President became wild with excitement, but the moment General Grant walked through the door, the crowd grew still and parted like the Red Sea for the general's passage towards President Lincoln.

Senator Ross said that when the two great men met for that first time they shook hands with obvious pleasure, and then the President's Secretary of State, Mr. William Seward, took the general over to introduce him to Mrs. Lincoln. As General Grant and Mrs. Lincoln walked about the room, the crowd became frenzied with excitement. Men and women cheered and pushed forward to better see the general, to pound his back and shake his hand. Ladies' dresses were stepped on and torn and many women climbed onto tables and chairs to escape further harm.

Above the chaos, loud voices demanded that General Grant stand up so as to be better seen. With obvious reluctance he stood on a crimson sofa while perspiration spotted his face and veins popped out on his forehead. After a long, embarrassed moment of being a spectacle for the crowd, General

Grant welcomed help to flee from the room, but even after he had escaped, his name was cheered and shouted.

Senator Ross paused in the telling of his story, and smiling sheepishly he admitted that he had added his own voice to the ruckus, for he said that Grant's face gave him hope. In the lines of Grant's weathered face, he recognized Victory and Reunification and Peace.

Tomorrow President Lincoln will officially name General Grant as the Lieutenant General of the Armies of the United States. Pa said the honor is great—the rank had to be voted on by both the House of Representatives and the Senate and approved by President Lincoln. There have been only two other lieutenant generals in our country's long history, one of whom was George Washington! Pa said that General Grant deserves this honor for having proven himself mightily on the battlefield.

Regina, in one short day General Grant has accomplished much—he has told me that my music does help the soldiers and thus fulfills my vow to help Mr. Lincoln's Great Cause—he has shown my sister, Mary, that successful men can remain modest and humble—and he has given Senator Ross new hope that our Union will be preserved. Imagine, dear friend, what General Grant will accomplish in the coming days as the Supreme Commander of all our Nation's armies.

Saturday, April 2

Regina, I am pleased you wish to learn more about sculpting a bust! Before I even begin my work I must envision what the finished piece will look like. After all, dear friend, a sculpture is not merely a duplication of someone, it is, in the end, a creation all of itself.

After my vision becomes clear, I place before me an aperture, which is a coil of wire shaped like the head of my subject.
That oval of hollow wire is mounted on a pole and planted in
a square of wood so that it stands upright. I fill the oval with
clay and then begin adding bits of clay to build up the shape
of my subject's head. Once that is completed I sculpt the face
and hair by using an assortment of tools to add or remove clay.

I prefer to have my subjects sit for me, but I have sculpted
some busts based on pencil sketches. If I work from drawings, I
first sketch that person from every angle—from behind, in
front, to the sides, and even from above—because the sculpture, when finished, will be viewed from every angle.

One of my projects is a bust of Mr. Lincoln. Thus far I am
displeased by my work on his head, for I have failed to capture
his unique features. It is near impossible to sculpt his face by
studying his image in newspapers. My dearest ambition, Regina,
is to sit near him and sculpt his face in clay.

I must close this letter now, for my arms and hands ache terribly. Today, at the studio, I kneaded grogged clay for three long
hours.

Tuesday, May 3
Tonight my family accompanied me to Lincoln General Hospital, where I performed in the Grand Concert. It was a wondrous
affair attended by gowned ladies and gentlemen in evening attire
and officers, sailors, and soldiers in crisp uniforms.

While waiting nervously with the other performers behind
the curtain, I came upon James Kilmar. We greeted each other
fondly and then he patiently answered all my questions about
his studies at the Peabody Conservatory. He looked wonderful—taller than I remembered and quite handsome, especially

when he smiled, which was often. He wore a curved brass hook at the end of each arm, and despite the cumbersome appearance of those hooks he managed quite nicely to remove his hat and unroll his satchel of sheet music.

James performed during the first hour. While he sang, his voice floated around the hall with a beauty not of this earth. He sang in Italian, an operatic piece I believe, and after he had finished the audience rose to their feet and thundered applause. Through the curtain I spied Mrs. Kilmar clapping wildly, her eyes on her son's joyous face.

For my turn on stage I sang the ballad "Annie Laurie" as a surprise for Ma, for that song reminds her of her beloved Scotland. Pa told me later that after my song ended and the audience kindly showed their appreciation, Ma's proud smile lit up the darkened theatre like a torch in the night.

But then, Regina, I disgraced myself completely. I sang a duet with a sweet girl named Emma Bartlet. We sang a lovely piece, "No, Ne'er Can Thy Home Be Mine," and when we reached the second stanza I sang horribly off-key. I was mortally embarrassed. Mary said my cheeks burned so red that she pitied me, but she was proud that I carried on and completed the song with Emma.

Afterwards, backstage, I apologized profusely to Emma, but I couldn't tell her the true reason why my voice had faltered and fallen flat. I shall tell you the reason, dear friend, for I know you will understand.

Yesterday, Pa met an old friend from Arkansas who told him news of our former neighbors in Fort Smith. He told Pa that Boudy resigned his rank as a lieutenant colonel in the Confederate Army when he was elected by the Indian Territory to serve as a delegate to the Confederate Congress.

Oh, Regina, Boudy's decision to support the Confederate

cause still troubles me, and yet he invades my every thought every hour of every day! Tonight, when Emma and I performed our duet and I sang the words "Thou wilt have scorn for me," I thought suddenly of Boudy—surely he has nothing but scorn for me. In that very instant my heart splintered into tiny pieces and my voice betrayed me. I fear that my criticism of his beloved Confederacy has dried up his heart. Oh, Regina, I fear that his love has drifted like dust in the wind.

Wednesday, May 25

This evening began peacefully. Pa and Senator Ross were at the stables tending to the senator's lame horse and Mary was at the theatre with one of her beaux. I was content sitting by the hearth looking through my scrapbook, pasting in newspaper articles about recent battles and the re-election campaign of Mr. Lincoln. Ma was sitting on the sofa knitting, as she often does on these quiet nights.

A brisk knock at the door startled us and I hurried over to see who our visitor was. A worn-looking soldier stood there with an envelope in his hand. He asked my name; satisfied by my answer, he said he had a missive for my mother. Then, tipping his hat, he walked off into the night.

The envelope was small, though heavy, which puzzled Ma. When she slit open the flap a coin fell out—a silver dollar with a dent in its center. We recognized the coin at once as belonging to Nathan Ennis. Ma read the letter he had enclosed, and then with tears spilling from her eyes she handed the note to me.

Nathan's letter was dated May 4. He wrote:

Dear Mrs. Ream,

Tomorrow we fight in a thick woods called the Wilderness.

Last year we fought in those same dark woods during the battle of Chancellorsville when Bobby Lee's army whipped our army under General Joe Hooker. This time around we have General Grant to command us, so we are bound to be victorious—if so, we will march on to Richmond. If we can then seize the Rebels' capital, this war will surely end.

Mrs. Ream, it is easier for me to write than to speak my mind. When last I visited your home I had hoped to find the courage to tell you what my pen now tells.

I told you once that my ma died when I was a babe. Pap refused to talk about her and so I never knew nothing about Ma. I used to wonder if she laughed loud or soft or if she liked to sing or if she could read. I always pictured her pretty with a kindly voice and gentle blue eyes and a goodly heart. Mrs. Ream, you come mighty close to the mother I always pictured.

I asked my fellow soldiers to deliver this letter and coin to you if something should happen to me—delivery of this letter means that I am dead.

Please remember me with fondness,
Nathan Ennis
P.S. I pray your son, Bob, returns home safe and sound.

Ma trembled with her grief and I thought for the thousandth time that Wars are especially sorrowful for mothers. I placed my arms around her and after a long while she asked me to bring her my scrapbook. She flipped through the pages until she found the account of the battle in the Wilderness, but her eyes were too tear-blurred to read and so I gently pulled my book from her hands and offered to read out loud.

After I had poured her a cup of tea and wrapped a warm shawl around her shoulders, I read about the battle that had claimed Nathan's life. My voice often broke with sadness, for I, too, had become fond of the shy soldier.

Regina, the battle in the Wilderness took place a few weeks ago, on the fifth and sixth of May—this is the second time our army has fought there. The Wilderness sounds like a dreadful place, for it is a dark forest scarred with twisted thickets and pieced with soggy patches of swampland. Beneath the shadows of towering pines and amidst tangled trunks of oaks and cedar and bushes of thorns, those soldiers of the Union and the Confederacy struggled to find each other. Blinded by the screening brush and choked by the smoke of fires and discharged weapons, the soldiers often lost sight of their own lines and fired upon their own men. Thousands fought, thousands died, and thousands were wounded. Even after the rifles had been silenced by the fall of night, hundreds of wounded soldiers were burnt to death by forest fires that were sparked during the fury of fighting. And yet, at battle's end, General Grant couldn't allow his tired men to rest, so he advanced them quickly to a hamlet in Virginia called Spotsylvania. There, on another field of blood, Grant's army clashed with Lee's for ten long days.

Regina, as I read Ma all this she sat very quietly, the silver coin clasped in her hand. My heart grieved to see her so distressed, but I didn't know what to say to lessen her grief, so I simply laid my head upon her shoulder. After some time Ma said in a bare whisper, "I wish Nathan had told me that he thought of me as his mother ... I would have told that dear boy that I thought of him as my son."

Saturday, June 25

My brother has sent a long letter. At the beginning of this month he fought in that slaughterous battle that took place at

Cold Harbor, Virginia. Bob wrote that the Union's assaults were suicidal, for the Confederates were well protected by stone works and trenches, and within a half hour thousands of Federals had fallen. As the noon hour passed, neither Lee nor Grant called for a truce to collect the wounded and dead, so throughout the afternoon the two armies stared at each other while between them the men of the South and the North lay dying. Within hours many wounded perished under the hot sun, for they had neither water for their thirst nor bandages for their wounds.

Oh, Regina, Bob admitted much more in his letter. He wrote that one side of his face is scarred from a bout of chicken pox, but at least he was luckier than most, for he survived the deadly disease. Bob admitted that he has been seriously ill at least four other times—once from eating meat infested with worms, once from drinking green swamp water, once from falling into a ditch of raw sewage, and once from malaria. He admitted, too, that he has been wounded twice—the first time when he met Nathan Ennis, and the other time when a bayonet pierced his leg (his leg is scarred, but because he avoided the surgeon he was spared amputation).

He wrote that he has no shoes. His bare feet are covered with blisters and cuts, and his greatest worry is to find boots before the snows of winter. Some of his fellow soldiers plunder shoes from the dead, but Bob hopes to buy boots before he, too, must resort to stealing from corpses. And he wrote that his uniform hangs like a rag on his back; on hot days the sun burns his skin red and on cold nights the wind chills him.

He wrote that he now gambles, for that is how he earns food. If my brother has luck with the cards or dice his stomach is full, but if he's unlucky he must dig up wild roots or snare rabbits and squirrel.

He wrote that he itches all the time, for fleas live in his clothes and lice nest in his hair. He rarely finds clean water and soap for bathing, so his body is caked with dirt and his teeth feel slimy and gritty. And he wrote of his exhaustion; deep sleep is impossible, for the nights are alive with sounds—the groans of the injured, the discharge of weapons, the screams of soldiers' frightening dreams, or the rustling of rats crawling over him.

Bob wrote all this and more, and then in large letters he told us that in spite of the hunger and cold and rats he would follow General Robert E. Lee into battle even if it meant certain death.

What kind of man is Lee, I asked Pa, that he can make my brother bear his deprivations with gladness? Pa said that Lee reminds him of a chivalrous knight in one of those old English tales, for he has courtly manners and a genteel voice. He carries himself tall, proudly, like a person of nobility. And yet, Regina, despite his gentility and gentlemanly manners, General Lee is known for his ferocity on the battlefield.

In my scrapbook I have a newspaper image of General Robert E. Lee. I think him handsome, for he has a fine white beard and a distinguished crop of white hair. Intelligence flashes in his eyes, and the cut of his chin is strong and regal. His mouth is determined-looking and yet reveals no sign of cruelty, for his face is marked by nobility, a nobility rarely seen in a soldier. Perhaps General Lee cannot be defeated because he is a general who understands the nature of War, and because he is a man whom other men follow willingly.

Friday, July 22

Congratulations on your graduation—how marvelous that you are now teaching French and Art for your uncle. The academy will be enriched by your knowledge and enthusiasm, Regina.

I share your disappointment that this War delays your Grand Tour, but peace shall come one day and then your dream to visit London and Paris and Salzburg will be possible. I, too, dream of visiting Europe, of studying sculpting in Rome, but of course that is an impossible dream for me as my parents remain poor. Regina, you must live our dream for both of us—after the War ends you must travel abroad and write me long, descriptive letters so that I can view the aged cities of Europe through your eyes.

Of late, I am much disturbed by General McClellan's bid for the Presidency—do you remember him, Regina, and how he was relieved of his command after Antietam? (Pa said Mr. Lincoln blamed McClellan for the thousands of lives that were lost that day.) McClellan, or Little Mac as he is known here in Washington, is gaining the support of those who are tired of War. He scorns General Grant, since he hasn't as yet defeated General Lee, and he points a finger of blame at Mr. Lincoln. Little Mac is predicting that the North will lose the Struggle, and thus he argues for an immediate truce between North and South.

Regina, Little Mac has publicly stated that he believes Mr. Lincoln was wrong to interfere with the institution of slavery. If the unthinkable happens and Little Mac wins the election, would he undo Mr. Lincoln's Emancipation Proclamation? Would he return freed men to slavery's chains?

My heart is dark with dread.

Saturday, August 13

This morning, while Ma and I baked bread, we noticed that a wagon had broken down in the alley behind our back door.

While the driver repaired the split wheel, his wife lifted down four children—four Negro children. The children were bone-thin and dressed in new clothes that hung on their stick arms and legs. I doubt they knew how to smile, for their mouths and eyes looked old, as though they had forgotten how to smile a century of suffering ago.

The lady explained that the children, all four of them sisters, had only just arrived in freedom through the Underground Railroad. Ma invited the lady and children into our parlor for tea and biscuits. Although the invitation was gratefully accepted by the lady, the children hesitated as though they mistrusted us. I carried the youngest child, a girl of perhaps four years, up the steps. She was pretty, though scarred, for she was missing her right ear. I was told in a whisper that the child's master had cut off her ear for the crime of eavesdropping.

Two of the sisters, twins of perhaps ten years, wouldn't accept the biscuits Ma offered them, so she placed the plates on their laps. After a while one twin touched a biscuit with her finger and then looked quickly at Ma, and when she smiled the little girl ate hungrily. Her bravery encouraged the others to eat.

While we spoke, the oldest child, a girl of twelve years, wept quietly, and we learned that she didn't understand that she had reached freedom. Later, when the wagon rumbled away, the little girl still wept. I doubt, Regina, that I shall ever forget the sound of her weeping.

Saturday, August 20

Throughout supper tonight, Pa was unusually quiet and ate absent-mindedly as though unaware he was eating. Ma and Mary noticed, too, and we asked Pa what troubled him. Sighing sadly, he said, "Mr. Lincoln is losing his bid for re-election."

My heart sank at Pa's words. The only threat to President Lincoln's winning the election is George McClellan—Little Mac continues to blame Mr. Lincoln for the War, and many, too many, are listening to his words. Little Mac's promise to end the War appeals to many voters, but don't they understand that as President, he would allow our Nation to remain divided into two separate countries?

Thursday, September 1
Tonight the front door was thrown open and Senator Ross bounded into our dining room, dropped down into a chair, and wiped at his red face with a kerchief. Finally he managed to say that General Tecumseh Sherman sent Mr. Lincoln a telegram that read, "Atlanta is ours, and fairly won."

At those words Pa whooped and the senator joined in with a holler and a ruckus as though they were children at sport. Ma begged to know why the fall of a Southern city caused them such glee, and Pa explained: the fall of Atlanta means that the Confederacy will lose the War and Mr. Lincoln will surely win the election!

You should have heard the noise we all made as we screamed and cried and laughed and cheered. When we had calmed ourselves, Senator Ross told us that with Atlanta's fall the Confederacy has lost both its manufacturing center and its center for Southern railroads. Now General Grant has only one more city to conquer to end this terrible War—the Confederates' capital of Richmond.

Oh, Regina, soon our Union will be reunited and never again will slavery darken our land. My heart feels as colorful as a rainbow.

1 8 6 4

Saturday, September 24

This is the first birthday I can remember that has closed in sadness. I have hidden my despair from Pa, Ma, and Mary, for they planned a lovely dinner and gave me gifts I'll treasure always, but I sit here in my attic with tears in my eyes.

My tears are tears of frustration. For several months I have been working on my bust of Mr. Lincoln, and every day my displeasure grows. I cannot capture his face as I wish, for I am forced to work from images cut from newspapers and they fail to reveal the details that a sculptor needs.

Today, at the studio, Mr. Mills looked over my scrapbook of sketches and asked why I hadn't saved newspaper caricatures of our President. I was shocked that he would think I'd keep those ugly cartoons drawn by Mr. Lincoln's enemies! I told him that I ignore every lampoon of Mr. Lincoln I see, for I detest drawings that depict him as a baboon or a backwoodsman or a slovenly, ugly creature. Mr. Mills is of the opinion that I am wrong to ignore the caricatures. He said that each caricature has value, for each one points out a different feature of Mr. Lincoln's face and personality. Reminding me of his own admiration for our President, Mr. Mills told me he has saved every caricature he has seen.

He pulled out a box from under a table and from it took a portfolio stuffed with newspaper clippings. We sorted through the clippings, choosing lampoons of Mr. Lincoln that would help me in the study of his face. Though the critical cartoons angered me, I had to agree that each sketch emphasized a different trait of Mr. Lincoln.

And so I sit here, Regina, studying these ugly cartoons that ridicule and taunt our good President, but I still cannot determine the texture of Mr. Lincoln's hair, or the deepness of the lines etching his face, or the exact width of his nose and eyebrows, chin and mouth.

The only feature I clearly see in the drawings is Mr. Lincoln's expression of sadness. Indeed, I have never found a picture in which he is smiling. It is his sadness that I hope to capture, for if I can't, then my sculpture will never take on a life of its own. And yet how can I add sadness to a face that I don't know well enough to sculpt?

Regina, before I close this letter I must protest your decision not to receive gentleman callers. Edward would never have wanted you to isolate yourself from the world. Please reconsider and allow gentlemen to call. You mentioned one in particular—the army officer Captain O'Brien. His work as an architect in a city as grand as New York City would fuel interesting conversations, I am certain.

P.S.—How rude of me not to have mentioned your birthday gift. Such a beautiful pouch for my combs! Your embroidery is exquisite, as always—the garland of flowers reminds me of spring. Thank you, dear friend, for remembering me.

Thursday, October 27

This afternoon Mr. Mills suggested that I attend one of Mr. Lincoln's public receptions so as to study his face and finish my sculpture. Before supper I asked Ma to chaperone me, and she readily agreed. We dressed with great care for our visit. I wore my Scottish gingham dress and rose hat, and Ma looked lovely in her frock of forest green.

At the White House we were asked to remove our cloaks. I overheard another guest say that Sergeant Crook, Mr. Lincoln's bodyguard, requires the removal of street clothes because weapons could be hidden within bulky coats or cloaks. I shudder whenever I am reminded that our President is in constant danger.

Ma and I joined a long line of hundreds of people, all of whom were interesting to look upon. There was a rather stout lady who wore mink gloves with ruby buttons, and before her waited an elderly Negro woman leaning on a twisted cane of birch. There were gentlemen with black ties and ladies with silken gowns who mingled with maidens in bonnets of gingham and men in homespun cloth. And there were soldiers and sailors of every age in faded uniforms and officers in crisply pressed uniforms. All were different, and yet every face I looked upon was flushed with the excitement of meeting our beloved President.

As Ma and I moved slowly towards Mr. and Mrs. Lincoln I tried to keep his face in sight, but my short height was against me. I peered around the portly gentleman in front of me but saw nothing more than carpet and wall. After some time I heard the clatter of running feet as the Lincolns' young son, Tad, ran past. Suddenly he stopped to grin at another boy before tagging him and running off. Shrieking with laughter the two boys ran up and down the line, which clearly annoyed the lady with the ruby buttons. At one point Tad darted in front of me and stumbled over my foot. I looked at him and he at me before I stepped forward to block the other boy. As Tad escaped he shouted out his thanks.

Finally Ma and I stood before Mr. Lincoln. I gasped as I looked up at him, for his height is great—after all, dear friend, I am but four feet, ten inches, and Mr. Lincoln measures near six feet, four inches tall! Wishing I had clay in my hand, I stared up at his wonderful face.

I bit my lip as Mrs. Lincoln turned towards me. I smelled

her perfume and heard the swishing of her petticoats just as the Marshall of the District of Columbia called out, "Mrs. Robert Ream, of Washington, D.C., and her daughter, Miss Vinnie Ream." At the sound of our names Ma and I stepped forward and offered our gloved hands to the Lincolns.

Mrs. Lincoln smiled wearily, but her greeting was warm. And then I offered my hand to Mr. Lincoln. Oh, Regina, my small hand was lost within his enormous gloved hand! He greeted me politely, but I can't remember what I said to him, or if I said anything at all, for shyness overcame me. In those few precious seconds I tried—oh, I tried so desperately hard—to memorize his eyes and his mouth and his nose and his hair, but my moment fled by and I walked away in a daze. I failed most miserably to learn enough about his face to complete my sculpture.

Oh, Regina, whatever shall I do?

Tuesday, November 1

As the day of election draws near, the butterflies in my stomach flit about as though in frenzied flight—Pa still believes the fall of Atlanta has won Mr. Lincoln the election, but Little Mac is boasting he'll win.

This afternoon I saw Mr. Lincoln walking with his son down Pennsylvania Avenue, the President's giant hand clutching Tad's small one. Boldly I followed them—at a respectable distance, of course—so as to study Mr. Lincoln's face. They soon turned down New York Avenue and into Mr. Stuntz's toy shop, a magical place that is forever Christmas. Mr. Stuntz speaks with a marvelous French accent. Indeed, he once served as a soldier in France and now his carvings of wooden soldiers are treasured by the boys of Washington. By the men as well, for it is said that Mr. Lincoln uses Mr. Stuntz's wooden soldiers to plan the battles of this War.

I spied through the shop's window and watched as Tad, after much deliberation, chose a toy soldier. Toy in hand, he smiled up at his father, who smiled too before placing coins on a counter. Moments later the door opened and they continued down the avenue. They hadn't walked far before a black carriage drew up beside them and a man leaned through the open window and spoke to Mr. Lincoln. I recognized the man at once as the Secretary of State, Mr. William Seward (Pa once told me that Mr. Seward is one of Mr. Lincoln's most trusted friends). Much to my disappointment they boarded the carriage and another opportunity to study Mr. Lincoln was lost.

Oh, Regina, my dream to sculpt Mr. Lincoln is my heart's fondest desire. Will my dream ever be realized?

Wednesday, November 9
Yesterday, Election Day, the sky was an unbroken piece of grey slate as I accompanied Pa to the voting place. Our walk was miserable, for winds pushed us to and fro and icy rain dripped down our necks. The streets of Washington were strangely empty as though the city had been deserted, except for soldiers who stood on guard. Pa explained that troops were positioned throughout our city and the other great cities of our Nation, for it was feared that mobs who supported Little Mac would disrupt the election.

When Pa emerged from the voting place he was smiling, but I wasn't fooled by his cheeriness as we rushed home through the rain. My family spent the rest of the day in quiet. Mary has a sore throat and so she rested on the sofa by the hearth, with hot bricks at her feet and blankets piled around her. Ma sat near the hearth and read to Mary from their favorite novel,

Jane Eyre, while Pa spent the day working at the kitchen table on a map of Richmond.

Regina, I haven't told you before because I didn't want you to think me a braggart, but I have already completed several busts of prominent Washingtonians and all of them have been deemed successful by Mr. Mills. I have been paid handsomely for my work, which is of wondrous help to Ma's budget, but I remain frustrated with myself as a sculptress because I have failed to sculpt Mr. Lincoln. I spent yesterday as I often spend my free time—studying newspaper images of him in a vain attempt to determine the width of his jawbone and the thickness of his hair and the depth of his eyes.

During supper the skies blackened as winds howled around our house and rain pelted our windows. The storm frightened Ma, for she has many superstitions and most of them are about storms. Believing that the storm was a sign that Mr. Lincoln was doomed, Ma recounted numerous tales of Scottish lords who had lost castles or ships or ladies when the winds moaned and drowning rains fell.

After our sombre meal we joined Mary by the hearth and began a long wait for Senator Ross's return home—the senator, in the company of Mr. Lincoln, would learn before the newspapers did the outcome of the election.

Several hours past midnight we heard the senator's step at our door. His radiant smile told us at once what we had hoped to learn—that Mr. Lincoln will remain as our President. Ma wept with joy while Mary and I filled glasses with vanilla ice cream for a small celebration. As we ate, Senator Ross told us of his night.

He and a small company of men had gathered with Mr. Lincoln at the War Department, where they waited for the telegrams reporting the results from polls across our Nation. The violence of the storm slowed the telegraph wires, but eventually the telegrams began to pass through. President Lincoln read each one quickly before carrying on with his telling of anecdotes and jokes. Often he picked up a book of jests and read aloud to the company, but it was clear that he was anxious as he read the telegrams that arrived every few minutes.

Around midnight, Senator Ross told us, the telegrams indicated that President Lincoln had won the election. He took the news calmly, but with obvious relief that the American people still have faith in him as their leader. Modestly he accepted the congratulations of his friends before inviting them to join him for a late supper. Indeed, Mr. Lincoln himself spooned out fried oysters to his company.

After nearly two hours of eating and discussing important issues, Mr. Lincoln rose from the table to leave, but outside the door he was met by a brass band and a noisy crowd cheering his name and demanding a speech. Mr. Lincoln expressed his keen desire to return home to his wife, but he spoke a few words that Senator Ross said revealed the goodness of his heart. I asked the senator what Mr. Lincoln had said, and as far as I can remember, Regina, his words were thus: "I am thankful to God for this approval of the people ... but if I know my heart, my gratitude is free from any taint of personal triumph." Then Mr. Lincoln hurried off into the darkness, and Senator Ross came away home to tell us the good news of the victory.

Pa asked if there had been reports of protests or violence at any of our Nation's polls, but the senator shook his head no. Except for a few minor problems, Election Day passed peacefully and fairly. Just imagine, Regina, four million men voted and no one was attacked or murdered!

As we prepared to go upstairs to bed, Ma parted the drapes. Outside our windows the black sky was still starless, but the winds had calmed and rain no longer fell. Ma said, "finally the storm is over." I smiled happily at her words, for I realized that another storm has also ended—the storm over Mr. Lincoln's re-election. When I woke up this morning I was still smiling.

Thursday, November 10

Today I showed my finished sculpture of Mr. Lincoln to Mr. Mills, and as he inspected it I watched a frown deepen between his eyes. His frown told me that my work displeased him.

I knew Mr. Mills's criticism was just, for I had failed to capture the Sadness that marks Mr. Lincoln's face. As I struggled with my disappointment in myself, the door to the studio opened. Mr. Mills's guest was a familiar face to me, for it was Senator Trumbull, one of Pa's dearest friends. He had heard through Pa of my bust of Mr. Lincoln and was most curious to see it, but he noted instead my crestfallen face. Kindly, Mr. Mills explained the difficulties of sculpting a face rarely seen.

Senator Trumbull's brow wrinkled at that and he said, "Perhaps I should ask Mr. Lincoln to sit for you." I gasped, and grabbing his hands I implored him to indeed ask. Senator Trumbull laughed at my excitement. He asked Mr. Mills if I possessed the necessary talent to transfer Mr. Lincoln's face to clay, and Mr. Mills—bless him!—said yes.

Tonight at supper I barely ate, for all I could think about was Senator Trumbull's promise to speak on my behalf to Mr. Lincoln. Afterwards, my family and I put on our warmest coats and joined our neighbors in a jubilant march towards Pennsylvania Avenue. I carried a flickering lantern and Mary and Ma waved colorful banners. Pa walked between my sister and me so we could offer him the support he needed (his last bout of illness left him weak). Poor Mary had her own trouble walking, for she wore fashionable shoes that pinched her toes.

By the time we reached the lawns of the White House we were a grand, exuberant crowd. Cannons boomed in the near distance, which shook the many windows of the mansion. Through one window we spotted Tad Lincoln waving lanterns at us as a group of singers assembled under the President's portico and prettily sang for Mr. Lincoln to appear. I wanted to join the choir, but I hesitated leaving Pa, for he leaned on my arm heavily (clearly the walk had taxed him overmuch).

At long last, Mr. Lincoln stepped out onto the portico and the noise of our greeting filled up the heavens. Then quiet fell upon us all and in absolute stillness we listened as Mr. Lincoln spoke. Regina, there was one sentence he spoke that I will never forget. He said, "So long as I have been here I have not willingly planted a thorn in any man's bosom." That sentence revealed the goodness of Mr. Lincoln's heart. He went on to ask us to seek reconciliation with our Southern neighbors once the War ends. And he asked us to avoid revenge, for he said we should not "sully victory with harshness." Mr. Lincoln's speech ended with a request that we salute our soldiers, seamen, and all their commanders. We did as he asked, but then we added even louder cheers for him.

When my family returned home Ma insisted that Pa retire early. Upon awakening this morning he was much improved (his cough has all but disappeared).

Regina, our prayers for Mr. Lincoln's victory have been answered. Would God think me greedy if I asked Him another favor?—that I am granted permission by Mr. Lincoln to sculpt him.

Thursday, November 17

How I wish you lived across the street so I could knock on your door to tell you what passed this hour! Just minutes ago Senator Trumbull came calling. His face looked rather grim, and thus I knew he bore the dreadful news that President Lincoln had denied my request. The senator sat by our fire and accepted the tea Ma offered. I sat quietly beside Pa, but my heart pounded loud with disappointment.

After some moments of conversation, Senator Trumbull turned to me and said he had met with Mr. Lincoln and conveyed my keen desire to sculpt his head. While declining my request, Mr. Lincoln explained to the senator that he could not afford the time.

I bit on my lip, hard, to hold back my tears of disappointment as Senator Trumbull put down his cup. He told me that he then happened to mention that I was young and of humble origins, and at those words Mr. Lincoln scratched his neck and said, "That is to her credit." Senator Trumbull smiled then and told me that Mr. Lincoln will grant me a brief interview tomorrow to learn my intentions.

On hearing that, Regina, I felt my heart lift like a kite in the wind. I leapt to my feet and hugged Senator Trumbull. Ma was shocked by my forward behavior, but Pa laughed, for he understood my joy.

Dear friend, God listened to my prayers!

Friday, November 18

I am home from my meeting with Mr. Lincoln. I have pinched myself twice to ascertain that I am not walking in a dream.

Earlier today, a few minutes before the noon hour, Senator Trumbull and I knocked at the door of the White House. The doorkeeper took the senator's card and led us upstairs to the Lincolns' private quarters on the second floor.

At the end of a long hall he knocked softly and opened another door. Peering around the senator I saw President Lincoln sitting in a rocker. He sat in absolute stillness, his face turned towards an open window. As I looked upon him my heart trembled, for I saw on his face an expression of complete and utter sorrow. He didn't notice us standing there until a small white dog leapt from his lap and ran towards us with a fierce growl, though his tail wagged merrily.

President Lincoln rose then, and as he approached us he smiled and asked that we ignore his dog, Jip. Senator Trumbull introduced me, and Mr. Lincoln asked if I minded animals. I shook my head no. He smiled and said that his son—he calls him Taddie—has adopted every living creature he has found, and now a zoo of animals roams under the mansion's roof.

I laughed, for his story put me at ease, and so when he asked my purpose in seeking him out, I didn't hesitate—I told him that I wished to sculpt him. A frown knit his brows when he said, "Miss Ream, surely you can find a better subject than I, a homely man."

Regina, if I had been braver I would have told him that his face, though lined by years and coarsened by life, was beautified by his goodness. Instead I told him that I wished to sculpt him for the very same reason millions of men had voted for him. My answer must have quelled his curiosity, for he told me that he spends a half hour each day at noon resting at his desk. Oh, Regina, he gave me permission to sit in his office during that half hour to sculpt him—and he invited me to come every day except Sundays until my work is completed. I start tomorrow!

The interview ended then with abruptness. Senator Trumbull shook Mr. Lincoln's hand and I curtsied and bade him good-bye, but at the door I glanced around. Mr. Lincoln had sat back down in the rocker with his face turned once more towards the window. The smile he had shown me had faded, for his face was shadowed with unfathomable sorrow.

What does he look upon through that window, Regina, that could cause him such sadness?

Saturday, November 19

Last night I barely slept. My happy heart refused to calm itself; it beat madly like the wings of a hummingbird. In the morning, having ironed my gingham dress and readied myself, I went out on the street and hired a cartsman to bring my tools and clay to the White House. There, the doorman carried the tub of clay upstairs, and just as the noon hour struck, I was admitted into Mr. Lincoln's office.

President Lincoln greeted me cordially and indicated a closet that his wife had kindly emptied for the storage of my things, and then he sat behind his desk and opened a book. The only sounds in the room were the whisper of turning pages and Mr. Lincoln's occasional chuckles at what he read. He spoke not a word to me.

In absolute quiet I placed the stand in the corner and began to fill the hollow shape of the wire aperture with grogged clay. Filling in an aperture requires little concentration and so, as I pressed in handfuls of clay, I studied Mr. Lincoln's face.

I soon understood why the images of Mr. Lincoln had proved useless—images do him no justice. Perhaps the necessity of sitting without moving for nearly fifteen minutes for a photographer explains why Mr. Lincoln always appears stiff and stern in his images. Watching him as he read (a book of humor, I believe, for he laughed often), I noticed that his face changed and acquired a look of beauty. You must wonder, Regina, how I can call a man beautiful whom the world scorns as ugly, so I shall try to explain my meaning.

It is his eyes, Regina, that lend a gentle beauty to his rough face. His eyes are a luminous grey and deeply set under the shadow of bushy brows. His eyes speak of justice and goodness, and when he looks at you there is a dreamy quality as though he sees through you to your heart and reads what is written there. His eyes reveal patience and kindness, and thus, when you look at the rest of him, you see only a goodly man.

His head is covered by a dark thatch of wild, coarse-looking hair that seems as though it has never been combed or that he has just run his hand through it in a gesture of impatience.

His ears are large, as is his strong nose, but they fit well behind his dark beard. Deep lines crisscross his narrow forehead and edge either side of his nose. Perhaps, Regina, the lines scarring his face have been caused by the battles of this War.

His lips are full and wide—it is said that when Mr. Lincoln presses his lips together into a firm, straight line, it is a sign that he is determined and absolute in what he has just spoken. And when he speaks or laughs one can see large, very white teeth.

His hands are noticed at once, for they are huge and pow-erful-looking such as you would expect from a man who labored for thirteen years splitting rails with an axe. His shoulders slope, but there is the sense that no burden placed on his broad back would be too heavy. And he is lean, almost bony-looking, but again there is the sense that he has the strength to cope with any danger thrust against his Nation.

I disagree with the reports about his slovenly dress, for today he was clothed in a dark suit that even my fashionable sister would have approved of. His feet are huge, giant-looking, and today they were shod in shiny boots.

Regina, ignore the newspaper articles that label him a back-woodsman; he was that once, but surely it was his humble birth that bestowed upon him his sense of honor and dignity. If you could look upon his face as I did today, you too would see the gentleness, the goodness, that brightens his eyes with a tranquil beauty rare among men.

I must capture his expression—an expression of Sadness so deep that it is as though God were a stonemason and had taken His chisel and carved Sadness into Mr. Lincoln's face. Any sculptor could copy his eyes and his nose and his chin, but I want to capture God's carving.

Before I realized it, my half hour was nearing its end and I hurried to cover the aperture with a wet towel and place my apron and tools and tub of clay inside the closet. At half past twelve Mr. Lincoln closed his book and stood up. I bade him good day, curtsied, and left him rather pleased with me, I think, for keeping my promise not to overstay my welcome.

P.S.—I was delighted to read in your last letter that you now allow gentleman callers.

Thursday, November 24
When I entered the hallway leading to Mr. Lincoln's office today I heard shrieks of laughter, for Mr. Lincoln was running down the hall with his son perched on his back. Upon seeing me Mr. Lincoln bent forward so that Tad could hop down from his shoulders. The little boy looked up at me, squinted his grey eyes, and said, "You're the lady who helped me run away."

Mr. Lincoln looked puzzled, so I explained about the night at the open reception. He laughed and said he wondered what else went on at his receptions that he wasn't aware of.

We three went into the office then. Tad became my constant shadow—while Mr. Lincoln read his book, Tad plagued me with questions about the "mud" I was "playing with." I whispered that it was clay, not mud, and gave him a handful to shape, which mercifully kept him busy so I could finish filling in the aperture. By then my time was nearly over and so I covered the clay, put away my tools, and took my leave of Mr. Lincoln. As I walked downstairs I was followed by my little shadow and his many, many questions.

Tad is a darling boy, Regina, with his dark looks and his roundish face, but I dearly hope he is not present at every session or I will never finish my work.

Tuesday, November 29

Today, as always, I sat in my corner of Mr. Lincoln's office and carefully unwrapped the wet towels around the aperture. The shape of the head still displeased me. Using my wedging knife I sliced off large pieces of clay while studying Mr. Lincoln's face.

Mr. Lincoln seemed unaware of my presence today, as though he dwelt in another world. He sat slouched in his chair, his huge feet pushed forward and his chin pressed into his chest. His face was etched with that Sorrow which I recognize now as a permanent part of his face.

Oh, Regina, except on those occasions when his wife or Tad is present, Mr. Lincoln rarely smiles. Perhaps these years of War have scarred his heart. This afternoon, while I put away my tools, I was tempted to tell Mr. Lincoln that the Sorrows of this War have scarred my heart too, but I dared not interrupt his private grieving.

Saturday, December 3

Sometimes I deliberately arrive at the White House before my appointed time so as to sit outside Mr. Lincoln's office and watch as military men, politicians, ambassadors, clergy, and civilians parade in and out of his door. Punctually at noon I am ushered inside, where I claim my corner, unwrap the towel-covered aperture, slip into my apron, and begin my work.

Except for that first week, when little Tad asked endless questions and poked his fingers into my tub of clay, I have worked without interruption. Even so, my work progresses slowly, since some of my time is spent preparing the clay and cleaning tools. The shape of Mr. Lincoln's head is beginning to satisfy me, though, and soon I will remove and add bits of clay to form his nose, eyes, chin, and mouth. His hair I will add lastly, and by then the clay will take on a life of its own.

Throughout my half-hour sessions I carefully study Mr. Lincoln's dear face. In previous letters I have described his expression of sorrow, but of late I have discovered that he owns two separate expressions of sorrow. The first is caused, as I have written to you, by his guilt about the sufferings that War has brought upon his people. Strangely, the second sorrowful expression is caused by a rather mysterious object—a window. Whenever Mr. Lincoln looks out the window of his office, anguish—pure anguish—suddenly covers his face like a mask. Pity wrenches my heart when he wears that awful mask.

I am puzzled, Regina. Often I have looked out that same window and have seen nothing more than the beauty of Virginia's winter-browned hills, the azure waters of the Potomac, and wide skies of blue with scudding white clouds. And yet looking at such serene beauty brings no hint of pleasure to Mr. Lincoln's face. Today, he was so broken by grief that he sank into the chair nearest the window and wept aloud. A strong man weeping is always a tragic thing to see, but never was there grief equal to Mr. Lincoln's.

Today, as he wept his giant tears, I quietly put away my things and closed the door behind me. Dear friend, what does Mr. Lincoln see out that window? What does he look upon that brings him such sorrow? I must solve this unhappy mystery.

Sunday, December 11

For several weeks Pa has suffered with his rheumatism and so he works on his maps at home. After my return from the White House I prepare our noonday meal and Pa shows me his maps while we eat.

Of late he had been marking a map of Georgia on which he traced the path taken by General Sherman's army. It seems, dear friend, that after General Sherman burned the city of Atlanta he began marching his army in a southeasterly direction towards the city of Savannah, a distance of three hundred miles. Each day Sherman's army marched twelve of those miles, and as they marched they cut a path sixty miles wide—a path of utter destruction as homes were burned, cattle were killed and left to rot, and fields were razed and torched. Pa's map shows that Sherman's path swept through Decatur and Covington, then passed west of Eatonton and continued on through Milledgeville, Sandersville, Tennille, and Millen.

How terrifying it must be, Regina, to be roused from one's bed and forced to watch helplessly as soldiers search through family treasures before setting one's home ablaze! Pa heard that the very air of Georgia smells with the stench of decay and fire, for Sherman is determined to destroy the South's last hope for victory. I pity the people of Georgia.

Yesterday, General Sherman reached the city of Savannah. Pa's map is finished. General Sherman has reached the sea.

Wednesday, December 14

I was delighted to read about your pleasant evening at the Cotillion. How wonderful that your dance card was fully filled out. I smiled when I read that Captain O'Brien had claimed every dance. Surely the gossip tongues of Missouri are still wagging about that! Forgive my teasing, Regina, for I am truly happy that you are mingling in society. Your aunt and uncle must be pleased by your decision to rejoin your circle of friends.

Your description of Captain Michael O'Brien portrays a most charming man. Honestly, do his eyes flash green when he laughs and does his smile chase the gloom from the corners of your heart? Honestly? If so, Regina dear, you have fallen in love and I rejoice with you. Don't despair that he has never mentioned matrimony, for he might be unaware of his own feelings. Ask for a lock of his hair and place it under your pillow and perhaps he will dream of you.

Mary has an unwanted beau, a gentleman named Mr. Percival Jerkins. He calls each evening on my sister, but she can't bear him for she says he reeks of pickles. Indeed he should, for he owns a pickle-processing plant.

For myself, there are gentlemen who call, but I have no heart to give. Boudy crowds my every thought. Once this War ends, do you think he will seek me out? How I regret that day long years ago when I sent him that letter admonishing him for his allegiance to the Confederacy! What a stupid child I was.

Wednesday, December 21

I made no progress on Mr. Lincoln's bust today, for he had

three interruptions.

The first visitor was a handsome woman who called on behalf of her only son, a soldier for the Confederacy who is imprisoned in Washington's Old Capitol Prison. A Presidential Pass was required for visits, and Mr. Lincoln graciously wrote out the pass even while he apologized that her son was "kept from his home." Grateful, the woman kissed Mr. Lincoln's hand, and as she hurried away I heard him murmur, "You have but one son while I still have two—my eldest, Robert, and my youngest, Tad."

A second visitor, a sweet girl of perhaps twenty years, curtsied prettily, but when Mr. Lincoln asked the nature of her errand her cheeks became pink and she was overcome with shyness. Mr. Lincoln smiled and said he could tell by her blushes that she wanted to see a sweetheart, and he wrote her a pass so she could visit his camp.

The third visitor delivered a telegram from General Tecumseh Sherman. Mr. Lincoln ripped open the missive and read it to himself, and then, glancing over at both me and the messenger, he told us that good news should be shared. In an excited voice he read, "'I beg to present you, as a Christmas gift, the city of Savannah.'"

Regina, Savannah belongs to the Union! This Terrible Conflict between our states will soon be over.

P.S.—I nearly forgot to answer your question—no, I don't think Captain O'Brien will leave for New York the moment the South surrenders. After all, he has declared his love for you!

Friday, December 23

Merry Christmas to you, to your aunt and uncle, and of course to your distinguished Captain O'Brien. May your holiday be blessed with joy.

The commissions I've earned from sculpting head portraits have allowed my family some luxuries this Christmas. Ma has long admired the German custom of fir trees, so this year we bought a small tree and adorned it with glass balls and candles. Also, for the first time we could afford store-bought gifts for those we love. I am giving Ma a lovely shawl and Pa a vest of plaid. For Mary I have found a feathered purse, and for my friends, Senators Ross and Trumbull and Mr. Mills, I bought boxes of Cuban cigars.

Washington is ablaze with the celebration of the holiday. For a short while we can all pretend there is no War and no suffering. Christmas geese, rum cakes, and gingerbread are displayed in every shop window, and the theatres are lit up throughout the night. Carolers claim every corner and even the sternest face is wreathed with a smile. Truly, it is impossible to keep Christmas from hearts—even hearts weary of War.

Saturday, Christmas Eve

Ma has sent me upstairs to my attic room to rest my voice (this afternoon I sang for the wounded in the Post Office hospital, and later, at midnight, I will sing with the choir at church), but I must write you this letter at once, for I have solved the mystery of Mr. Lincoln's window.

When I arrived today for my half hour at the White House. I was gladdened to see that Christmas had found its way even into the Lincolns' home. Tad should be allowed the merriment of the holiday in spite of those who criticize his parents for celebrating Christmas during War.

Mr. Lincoln seemed in a festive mood. While I sculpted he sat with his white dog, Jip, on his lap and fed him bits of cake. Several times Mr. Lincoln looked my way as though studying me, and after one especially long look he said, in a wistful voice, "I regret the necessity of saying that I have no daughters." Then he began to speak of his son Willie, of his gentle ways and of the fever that robbed him of life. And then, Regina, Mr. Lincoln said the most amazing thing—he said I bore a resemblance to his son, for Willie, too, was small and of an artistic nature. Upon saying that Mr. Lincoln grew quiet as he looked through his window.

My fingers skimmed over the clay, for I felt honored that our President should compare my nature to his son's nature, and later I flew out the door as though wings were strapped to my shoes. I was rushing through the front gate when I realized I had left my wedging tool on the floor, and so I hurried back upstairs to Mr. Lincoln's office. As I raised my hand to knock I saw through the open door our dear President standing by the window. Tears coursed down his face and at his side stood Mrs. Lincoln. Not wishing to intrude I turned to go, but Mr. Lincoln's words arrested my step. He said, "Every time I look out this window I imagine Willie at play and I am wrenched with pain. Unbearable pain ..."

Oh, Regina, the mystery of the window is clear to me now. When Mr. Lincoln looks out that window he sees neither Potomac waters nor blue skies and brown hills. Instead he imagines his beloved child, Willie, as he once was before his death, playing on the lawns beneath the window.

1865

Monday, January 2

My dear friend Regina,

Our New Year began quietly and peacefully until this morning. I had only just arrived at the Post Office when my manager,
Mr. Martin, handed me a letter discovered in a sack of mail
from Virginia, addressed to my parents. Noting my joy—the
handwriting was Bob's—Mr. Martin sent me home at once. Pa
was at the War Department, but Ma was home and in a trembling voice she read the letter out loud.

It was a clear warning that we might not recognize him upon
his return home. Bob wrote that he is bone-thin, for he has been
living for months on daily rations of a pint of parched corn. No
longer can he gamble for food, for there is none to be won, and
there is no leisurely time for snaring rabbits or wild birds.

Bob didn't write to complain about his hunger. Instead he
wrote to tell us what he could not admit to any of his fellow soldiers—if he did, he'd be court-martialed for disobeying an order.

Oh, Regina, Bob confided that he is under orders to shoot
soldiers deserting from the Confederate Army. He wrote that
as the deserters run, crawl, or even boldly walk past, he looks
upon their starved, sickly faces and he shoots as ordered, but
high above their heads. Bob doesn't label them cowards but
knows they run in fear of a rumor—a rumor that once Petersburg falls to General Grant, President Jefferson Davis will sue
Mr. Lincoln for peace. That rumor has reached the women of
the South and they have written letters of hardship begging
their men to desert without fear of dishonor. Bob understands
all that as he aims his gun over the heads of his fellow soldiers
and bids each of them a silent and fond farewell.

My brother ended his letter by vowing that he himself will
never desert the Confederacy—even though he disobeys orders

to shoot those who do flee, he will stand by his beloved General Robert E. Lee until the War ends in Surrender.

Dear friend, please pray that my brother returns home unharmed! Since reading his letter my mother has aged ten years.

Tuesday, February 14

I was delighted by your recent letter, especially by the news of your betrothal to Captain O'Brien. Surely you and Michael will know true happiness throughout your married life. How honored I will feel walking down the aisle as your Maiden-of-Honor.

Please, Regina, try not to worry yourself overmuch. I know I have often remarked in past years that the War would end soon, but this time I can say that with authority—truly the War is coming to an end and soon Michael will return to your side. When he does, decide on your Wedding Day and let me know at once, so that I can book passage on the fastest train to Missouri.

Your notion of sewing seed pearls across the bodice of your wedding gown is lovely. Perhaps you could sew pearls onto your veil as well. Have you decided what flowers you'll carry in your bouquet or what songs will be sung in the church? Have you decided where you will travel for your wedding trip? Will you live in New York City or stay in Missouri afterwards? Have you met Michael's parents (do Mr. and Mrs. O'Brien live in New York)?

Write to me quickly, Regina, and satisfy my curiosity, for I wish to share your exciting plans.

P.S.—Pa, Ma, Mary, and Senator Ross send their best wishes. Mary longs to plan her own wedding, but of late she hasn't met anyone she'd care to marry. Ma worries that Mary will become a spinster if she continues to reject proposals of marriage—she will soon be nineteen years of age!

Sunday, February 19

Pa always waits until I return from my sculpting session with Mr. Lincoln to share our noonday meal. Ever kind, Pa never fails to ask of my progress on the bust before we discuss the War.

This afternoon, as we sat by the hearth, a smoldering log burst and a fiery splinter flew out and touched my dress. As a tiny flame rippled across the cloth Pa leapt up from his chair, and although he could see that the flame had been smothered, his eyes were clouded with worry. I questioned his sudden concern over fire, and in a grave voice Pa told me this—two days ago a burning cotton bale sparked a wall of fire that has destroyed Columbia, the capital city of South Carolina. I knew of Columbia as a beautiful city of elegant mansions and magnificent parks. Horrified, I asked Pa to tell me more.

It seems, Regina, that General Sherman's army had been marching up the Carolinas towards Richmond. The march led through woods and swamps swarming with alligators and poisonous snakes and over rough and harsh land. As Sherman marched, his soldiers burned and destroyed all that lay in their path. Two nights ago, when Sherman's army reached Columbia, some Confederate soldiers may have set fire to a bale of cotton as they fled the city—or perhaps the fire was begun by Union soldiers as they entered the city. Strong winds swept the flames into a storm of fire that soon engulfed every street. It is said that thousands of citizens cringed along those burning streets, some screaming, some weeping, and some staring in silence. And it is said that General Sherman was so moved by the sight of mothers clutching children to their hearts that he worked alongside his soldiers as they tried, desperately, to control the fire. Their attempt was in vain. The flames reached an arsenal and a mighty explosion ignited more fires. By dawn, the city that once shone like a precious jewel of the South was changed into a city of ashen ruins. In one night, thousands of citizens have been impoverished.

Pa heard that General Sherman's army withdrew from Columbia today—his army is now marching towards Virginia to join forces with General Grant's army. Soon they will move on to Petersburg and end this War. I suppose we should be grateful that Sherman's March is speeding this War to an end, but tonight as I mended the scorched cloth of my dress I was reminded of those poor families of Columbia. No matter if Yankee or Rebel caused that inferno in Columbia, this War sparked that fire. Surely, War is the cruelest of all human creations.

Wednesday, March 1

This afternoon Mrs. Lincoln happened by as I began sculpting the locks of Mr. Lincoln's hair. I explained how the clay must be shaped to reveal her husband's coarse, thick hair, and she admired my effort. Then, quite suddenly, she asked if I am a believer in dreams. I admitted my belief and told her, as proof, that my constant dreams of sculpting Indian children predicted my career as a sculptress. My answer must have vexed her sorely, for with a swish of her skirt she angrily rushed off. Noting my embarrassment, Mr. Lincoln kindly explained that his wife is frightened by a dream that he recently had, and then, with even greater kindness, he confided his dream.

He dreamt he was woken by loud weeping; curious, he rose

from his bed. He wandered downstairs, and though he searched the rooms he saw no one even as the sounds of weeping increased. Puzzled, he searched on until he came to the East Room. There he saw a catafalque and on it rested a corpse wrapped in funeral vestments. A mob of people surrounded the corpse, which lay with its face covered. Mr. Lincoln went up to one of the soldiers guarding the corpse and asked, "Who is dead in the White House?" The soldier replied, "The President ... killed by an assassin." Suddenly the crowd wailed out loud and their anguished voices awoke Mr. Lincoln from his dream. He slept no more that night.

Oh, Regina, ice crusted my heart as he spoke, for his enemies have veins filled with venom instead of blood. My time was spent by then and so I wrapped wet towels around the bust and bade Mr. Lincoln farewell.

Even now I reason with myself that Mr. Lincoln's dream was merely a mirage of sleep, but the ice around my heart has refused to melt.

Saturday, March 4

Four years ago, when I was a mere child in Arkansas, I longed to attend Mr. Lincoln's first inauguration, but I lacked the necessary wings. Today I needed only my two feet to carry me to the steps of the Capitol for Mr. Lincoln's second Inaugural Address.

The grey skies threatened rain, but Mary and I wore our prettiest hats as we made our way along Pennsylvania Avenue. We had great difficulty walking, for thousands of people crowded the pavement. By the time we had pushed ourselves onto a step in front of the Capitol, the hems of our dresses were black with mud, our shoes were ruined from splashing through puddles, and the feathers on Mary's hat had been flattened by the rains (my sister still looked beautiful while I was a sodden sight).

As we waited for the ceremony to begin, Mary and I amused ourselves by looking at the faces of the crowd, which had claimed every bit of road and grass. We spotted Mr. Whittman, the coward who deserted Mary at the first battle of Bull Run (a thin girl—his wife, we believe—hung on his arm). We saw one of our neighbors and Mr. Donald Martin from the Post Office, a judge Pa knows, and the actor Mr. John Wilkes Booth. Mary thought him handsome, but his face appealed little to me, for it is rumored that his sympathies lie with the Confederacy.

After an eternity of waiting, the doors of the Capitol opened and the important men of our government and courts rushed out. In their midst strode Abraham Lincoln. The crowd roared its approval so loudly that I'd swear the very clouds shook in the heavens.

Regina, what happened next will stay in my memory forever. When Mr. Lincoln stepped forward to deliver his speech the grey skies parted and the sun burst through and illuminated his face. He stood there, tall and proud, within the circle of golden light while the crowd oohed and aahed. All around me I heard excited whispers that the sun on Mr. Lincoln's face was a premonition of Peace for our country—that the light was a sign of God's approval. Hushed, all listened as Mr. Lincoln spoke.

Dear friend, his final words have been engraved in my very soul, for he said,

With malice toward none; with charity for all ... let us strive on to finish the work we are in; to bind up the nation's

wounds; to care for him who shall have borne the battle and for his widow, and his orphan …

When he said those words I glanced around and saw men and women unashamed of the tears wetting their cheeks. Our thunderous applause assured Mr. Lincoln that we would do as he asked to bind up our Nation's wounds. Quiet came then as he placed his right hand on the Holy Book and spoke the Oath before kissing the Bible. At that moment cannons roared out, but I swear the roaring of my heart was louder as I watched Abraham Lincoln turn and walk back into the Capitol.

How I wish you could have been standing there beside me, Regina, to look upon the face of our President. How blessed this Nation is to have that Great and Wondrous Man as our Father for another four years!

Sunday, March 5

Last night I accepted the invitation of a young physician, a clever Scotsman named David MacPhail, to attend the President's Inaugural Reception at the White House. I wore a gown of white satin and crisscrossed my hair with ribbons of gold.

The mansion was elegantly decorated, but the hall was so overcrowded with thousands of well-wishers that the police permitted only a few to enter the East Room at one time. As we waited our turn in the hall, the heat became so unbearable that I felt quite faint. Indeed several ladies did faint, and since the doctor couldn't reach them, their unconscious bodies were passed over the heads of the crowd to windows and then carried along planks of wood to the ground. That is the only reason I refused to faint, Regina, for I would have been humiliated to be passed like a sack of potatoes through a window!

At last David and I were admitted into the East Room, where Mr. Lincoln had been standing for hours greeting guests. Over in a corner the Marine Band played, but the music only added to the noise. I looked over at Mr. Lincoln and thought him weary, for his face appeared grey with fatigue.

My escort and I moved slowly up the reception line towards Mr. Lincoln. A dozen paces ahead of me stood one of his friends, a gentleman I know as Mr. Noah Brooks, and when they shook hands I heard Mr. Lincoln shout, "Did you notice that sunburst? It made my heart jump." (Indeed, Regina, the sunlight that flooded Mr. Lincoln's face at the Inauguration made my heart jump too.)

As the line moved slowly on, all at once Mr. Lincoln straightened his sloped shoulders and stepped out of the reception line in front of a pretty girl and her beau, a lieutenant who was balancing himself on a crutch, for he had lost one leg. Mr. Lincoln stood before the startled pair, and taking the hand of the officer he said in the warmest of tones, "God bless you, my boy!"

As the soldier turned and passed by me I heard him murmur, "I'd lose another leg for a man like that!"

I had nearly reached Mr. Lincoln when a guard rushed up and spoke to the President in a lowered voice. Mr. Lincoln's reply boomed out, "Invite him here at once," and moments later a Negro gentleman walked through the door. Upon seeing him, Mr. Lincoln's face was lit by a broad smile as he shouted out over the noise of celebration, "Here comes my friend Douglass."

Regina, surely you've heard of the famous Mr. Frederick Douglass, the Abolitionist who speaks and writes so fluently about slavery—the gentleman was none other than he!

As Mr. Lincoln shook Mr. Douglass's hand with warmth, he

said, "Douglass, I saw you in the crowd today listening to my inaugural address. There is no man's opinion that I value more than yours. What do you think of it?"

Mr. Douglass replied with equal warmth, "Mr. Lincoln, it was a sacred effort."

P.S.—Tomorrow night Mary and I shall dance at the Inaugural Ball, for we have been invited by two dashing officers from the state of New York.

Tuesday, March 21

Today when I entered Mr. Lincoln's office a shadow fell across my heart. He nodded at me in greeting and then sat ever so quietly, his eyes narrowed with pain. At once I knew he was suffering from another headache, much like the excruciating headaches that have long plagued his good wife. After I had placed my tools on the table I inquired about his health. He admitted his weariness and told me that he and Mrs. Lincoln will spend a leisurely holiday visiting General Grant's headquarters at City Point, Virginia. Mrs. Lincoln is rather excited about the boat trip, for they will visit with their eldest son, Robert, who serves as a Captain under General Grant.

Have I mentioned Robert in my letters to you? I have met him but once, for a brief moment. He struck me as a rather sombre gentleman of fine appearance, for he is tall and dark of hair. I believe he is a graduate of Harvard's Law School. There is gossip that he is smitten with Senator Harlan's lovely daughter, Mary, and that Mrs. Lincoln hopes they marry.

Mr. and Mrs. Lincoln will leave on their boat trip this Sunday and shan't return to Washington until April 11. The next few weeks will seem empty without my visits to Mr. Lincoln's office. Dear friend, you can only imagine how I dread the day

my sculpture is finally completed and I must forsake the pleasure of his company.

P.S.—Perhaps I should allow that little scamp, Tad, to play
near the bust—if it were broken, I could start anew!

Monday, April 3
Tonight Senator Ross burst through our front door and wordlessly held up a newspaper. Pa snatched at the paper, and with
undisguised joy he read in a loud voice, "The Confederate capital of Richmond has fallen … President Lincoln is walking
down the streets of the city surrounded by freed slaves …"

Ma clutched at Pa's hands and as they embraced I heard my
mother sob out Bob's name. Oh, Regina, my brother might be
home soon, for surely the Confederates will have to surrender
now that Richmond belongs to the Union!

Senator Ross waited until my family had calmed enough to
tell us even more news—General Lee's army is marching west
out of Petersburg.

Petersburg! Pa once told me that entire city was surrounded
by trenches dug by both Union and Confederate hands.
Trenches! What a fancy word for deep, dank ditches infested
with rats and lice and all sorts of horrible things. Those
trenches should have been named graves. Now that the long
siege of Petersburg is at an end those brave soldiers can climb
out of those terrible holes.

The hour is growing late, but as I sit here by my attic windows I cannot sleep. Oh, Regina, though I rejoiced earlier
tonight, I am now troubled by disturbing thoughts.

Is my beloved brother still alive? If so, he is marching west
with General Lee's ragged army, and behind them marches the
army of General Grant, who is relentless in the pursuit of his

enemies. Oh, Regina, Bob must be alive and he must come home to Ma and all of us. And yet, will we know him or will he be a stranger to us? Will he be bitter about the defeat of the Confederacy? Will he still love my parents? My sister? Me?

I worry, too, about Boudy. What will become of him when President Davis' government is dissolved? Has the War changed him, too? Does his absence of letters mean that I am absent from his heart? Has he labeled me his enemy—a Unionist—a Yankee? Or has he simply forgotten me? Has his love melted like spring snow under a warm sun?

I'll close now, for I shall brew a pot of tea and sit with my mother by the hearth.

Wednesday, April 12

Pa came home early this evening with tears warming his eyes. Choking with emotion he said, "Bob will be home soon."

We understood Pa's meaning at once. The War is over! Oh, Regina, doesn't it seem miraculous that General Lee has finally surrendered his army to General Grant!

Ma made the most delicious supper of sausage pie and stewed carrots while Mary and I set the table with flowers and our finest china. Whistling, Pa dusted off a bottle of crab-apple wine he had been saving for this very day of celebration. Only Senator Ross sat in quiet as he stared at the image of his wife and children that he carries in his pocket watch.

After supper we walked through Washington. The streets were riotous with celebration as singing and dancing filled the night. Colorful fireworks lit up the dark sky with dazzling light and everywhere could be heard shouting and laughter.

Our house is quiet now, but we are too excited to sleep. Ma is poring over her cookbook looking for my brother's favorite recipes—she is determined to fatten him up the moment he arrives home. Pa and Senator Ross are sitting by the hearth discussing General Joe Johnston and the other Confederate generals who have not yet surrendered. Mary is furiously ironing the gowns that she'll wear to the festivities and dances of victory. And I sit here by my attic windows, watching the joyous mobs of people milling about on the street below.

My heart is doubly glad, for today marks the end of War and tomorrow I will again see Mr. Lincoln. I have sorely missed him these past two weeks while he was away. I am anxious to see once more the welcome in his eyes, for he never fails to look upon me as though I were his own daughter. My joy exhausts me. I shall close this letter now and turn to my prayers, for I am anxious to thank God.

Thursday, April 13

The newspaper published an image of yesterday's Surrender at Appomattox. Is it possible, Regina, that the appearances of the two generals revealed their hearts? The handsome, chivalrous soldier Robert E. Lee in his general's uniform reminded me of the aristocracy of the old South. And the rough-faced, common soldier Ulysses S. Grant, in his private's uniform soiled by the mud of battle, reminded me of the determination of the North for Reunification.

The story under the image lent me hope that our people will heed Mr. Lincoln's good advice to help each other while our Nation heals. Surely generosity was shown when the Confederates were permitted to keep their horses and mules, for they will be needed to till barren fields. And I am especially pleased that General Grant provided food for the starving soldiers of the Confederacy.

At the War Department Pa learned that once the papers of
Surrender were signed, General Lee mounted his grey charger
to return to his headquarters. As he galloped past he was saluted
by General Grant and his officers—not with military salutes,
but with polite tips of their hats as neighbors would give. General Lee also tipped his hat cordially at the men who were once
his enemies. Pa heard, too, that when the Confederates placed
their weapons on the ground, the Federals wept. No harsh
words were uttered at Appomattox.

Regina, today I had to push my way through the streets of
Washington—my every step was blocked by thousands of citi-
zens and soldiers dancing and singing and parading about, but
I was determined not to be late for my session with Mr. Lincoln.

When I arrived, Mr. Lincoln was standing at his window—
the window through which he imagines his son, Willie, at play.
When I saw him, Regina, I caught my breath, for he was the
picture of exhaustion. He stood with his shoulders slumped, his
chin lowered wearily onto his chest, his face pale with fatigue.
When he heard me at the door he glanced my way. His eyes
were weary, but they wore that familiar look of welcome I have
come to cherish. I curtsied and said, "Mr. Lincoln, thank you
for bringing us, your children, through these troubled times,"
but he lifted his giant hand as though to dismiss my thanks and
with a smile he said, "I am weary, my dear, and so I shall sit at
my desk while you work." Then, sitting heavily, he picked up
his Bible and read while I smoothed and wet the clay.

In truth, Regina, the bust is finished, but I could not bring
myself to admit that to Mr. Lincoln. Not yet. How I dread
tomorrow! How I shall hate bidding him farewell.

After I left Mr. Lincoln I joined an immense crowd of men,
women, and children circling the White House. Constantly

people cried out for President Lincoln, and he appeared several times on his portico and spoke. Not once did he belittle the South. The final time he instructed the band to play "Dixie," and in a strong voice he shouted, "It is good to show the Rebels that with us they will be free to hear it again."

Tonight Washington is ablaze with the lights of flickering bonfires, countless candles, and lanterns. Even the night sky is afire as whistling rockets streak overhead like slashes of colored lightning. The darkness of night is no more, for every window of every house and every building is aglow with golden lamplight. I must close now, for Mary is impatient to leave for the dances along Pennsylvania Avenue—we shall dance until the morning sun rises and adds its own brilliance to the lights of celebration.

Friday, April 14

This afternoon I spent my final half hour at the White House. Each passing minute caused my heart agony, for I dreaded what I finally said: "Mr. Lincoln, my work is finished."

He glanced up from his reading with a startled expression and then, coming over to me, he looked at the bust for a long moment. "So that is my face," he said with a laugh in his voice. "Do I look as sad as that?"

His question required no answer—I could not have answered him anyway, Regina, for misery had stolen my voice. I wanted to smash the clay so I could start anew, but of a sudden Mrs. Lincoln was there praising my work, which brought a smile to her husband's dear face. No matter how my sculpture is regarded I have been successful, for I have, though for the briefest of moments, covered his sad face with pleasure.

As I draped the bust with a wet towel I overheard Mrs. Lincoln ask her husband to take her for a carriage ride. She mentioned, too, their plans to attend a play this evening at Ford's Theatre. Neither seemed particularly happy about attending the play, but their remarks made it clear that they felt obligated to appear publicly.

As I was taking my leave of the Lincolns, Mrs. Lincoln invited me to return on the morrow to take tea with her. I accepted at once, for that will allow me the chance to boldly suggest a sculpture of her head.

Tonight a strange sight occurred in the skies. Ma was outside sweeping the step when she happened to look up, and what she saw chilled her heart. She rushed inside, screaming, "There is blood on the moon, there is blood on the moon!" Pa and I hurried outside to see, but the moon had been swallowed up by the clouds of night.

Ma would not be calmed. We made her stand by the window and when the clouds released the moon we pointed out its whiteness, but she insisted that she had seen blood. Pa dislikes Ma's superstitions. To put her mind at ease he has suggested that they take a stroll under the white moon.

I must end this letter abruptly, Regina, for Pa and Ma will take it and drop it through the slotted door of the Post Office. After my parents leave for their walk I shall enjoy my privacy— first I must shampoo, but while I sit by the hearth and dry my hair, I plan to cut out images of wild birds and paste them into a blue scrapbook that Pa has given me.

P.S.—I forgot to tell you—Mary is at the same theatre as the Lincolns! Her escort, a remarkable officer who served under General Grant, raved about the play they will see—*Our American Cousin*, a British comedy with that marvelous actress Miss Laura Keene. I do hope Mr. Lincoln has a pleasant evening— he is fond of comedies and sorely in need of laughter.

Saturday, April 15

I am sitting by my attic window, looking down upon the city, a city crazed with anger and anguish. Thousands are roaming the streets looking for one man. One terrible man. Rain is falling. Nature is weeping. Our Dearest Friend is gone.

Oh, Regina, it seems incredible that only hours ago I was contentedly sitting by the hearth with my book and scissors. As I opened the door upon my parents' return from their walk, a man ran past, shouting, "Lincoln has been shot!" We stared in disbelief, but a moment later a carriage drew up and Mary leapt to the ground and flew into Pa's arms, sobbing hysterically. Before Mary's escort sped off he shouted that it was true, that Mr. Lincoln had been shot. My legs weakened, but all at once Ma's strong arm was around me and we followed Pa and Mary inside.

Mary sat in Pa's rocker and with Ma's shawl around her shoulders her tremors soon ceased, but when she began to speak her voice trembled.

My sister said the play had already begun when Mr. and Mrs. Lincoln entered their box above the stage. Accompanying the Lincolns was a handsome couple that Mary recognized as Miss Clara Harris and her fiancé, Major Henry Rathbone.

My sister was delighted to see how close to the Lincolns she was seated. Though their box was draped, she could spy on them through the slit in their curtains and had a clear view of Mr. Lincoln in a rocking chair and his wife close by his side. Mary said it was a pretty sight to see Mrs. Lincoln resting her head on her husband's shoulder. They looked the happy couple, whispering to each other often and laughing at the comic performers. At one point the box must have grown chilly, for Mr. Lincoln stood up and put on his overcoat.

During the third act Mary happened to glance over at the Lincolns' box—Mrs. Lincoln had turned her face up towards her husband and Mary saw him smile down at her. Then the whole world went mad. Of a sudden there came the sharp sound of a pistol firing. Mary thought the gunshot was part of the play as a man leapt from the Lincolns' box to the stage. Perhaps the spur of his boot caught in the decorative banner, for he fell to the stage floor awkwardly, landing on his left foot and knee. Mary watched as he struggled to his feet and shouted, "Sic semper tyrannis!" while waving a dagger above his head. The floodlights glittered upon the steel of the blade—the blade was red with blood.

My sister recognized the man at once as the actor John Wilkes Booth—the man who had walked past us at Mr. Lincoln's inauguration. His words and gestures seemed out of place, but because he was an actor she reasoned that his dramatic leap to the stage was part of the play. The entire audience must have shared my sister's confusion as Booth turned and limped off the stage.

From the Lincolns' box came much commotion. Mary turned and saw Mr. Lincoln slumped down in the rocker, his head limp upon his chest. His wife stood over him, screamed, and then crumpled at her husband's feet. Someone in the theatre yelled, "What's the matter?" and Miss Harris shouted back, "The President is shot! ... Stop that man."

In that very second the audience erupted into pandemonium, people spilling from seats and aisles and stage. A congressman climbed on his chair and blasphemed the name of John Wilkes Booth. Other men cursed Booth's name and shouted, "Kill him!" while women wept and shrieked and fainted. Everyone ran about the theatre as though their hearts had burst, and Mary found herself pressed up against the stage in mortal danger of being crushed. Someone lifted her up onto the stage, where she crouched behind the gaslights as the actress Laura Keene stepped in front of her and begged composure from the audience. In the frenzy, my sister stepped up on the footlights and looked over at the Lincolns' box.

Major Rathbone stood there, red blood gushing down his arm, for Booth had stabbed him. Two men—doctors, my sister believes—leaned over President Lincoln. After some minutes the doctors and four soldiers lifted the President and carried him through the narrow door of the box. Behind them followed Mrs. Lincoln, supported by Major Rathbone, though blood still poured down his arm.

Mary and her escort forced their way through the mob until they stood on the street outside. There, a Lieutenant was wielding his sword to force back the frantic throngs pressing around Mr. Lincoln's stretcher. Across the street, on the stoop of a house, a man with a candle beckoned the doctors to make use of his home.

Mary said that within minutes thousands of angry people mobbed the street. Many shouted, "Burn down Ford's Theatre," and torches glared in the night until soldiers extinguished the fires. Near Mary stood a foolish man who yelled that he was glad Mr. Lincoln had been shot. Furious men caught him up and threw a noose over a lamppost to hang him. The police cut the man down and he disappeared into the crowd, the rope still hanging from his neck. It was then that Mary's escort brought her home, for he wished to join the search for John Wilkes Booth.

After Mary fell silent, we sat numbed by what we had heard. We sat like that for hours, wordless, motionless, lifeless, as the fire faded in the hearth and morning broke with rain. We sat there as the front door opened and slow footsteps sounded in the hall. It was Senator Ross. Seeing us gathered by the cold hearth, he said, "Abraham Lincoln is dead."

For a long while the only sound was the tapping of rain against our windows. Then Ma said, "Last night blood covered the moon. I knew Death would come."

Mr. Lincoln's body has been taken to the White House. Behind his coffin marched officers of his army, their heads bared in respect. Grief-stricken people lined the streets, and when the procession reached the White House, it was met by former slaves, weeping in the rain for their Great Emancipator. As Senator Ross told us all that, Ma and Mary began to weep, too, but my own eyes remained swollen with unreleased tears. I couldn't weep, Regina. I couldn't move as I watched the rain strike our windows.

The pen in my hand moves of its own free will. I have little strength. Sorrow has robbed me of strength. My heart no longer beats. Oh, Regina, Abraham Lincoln has left us. My dear Mr. Lincoln is gone.

Monday, April 17

Today I returned to the White House and pleaded for permission to take away my sculpture. I worried that when Mr. Johnson took over as our new President he would order the office cleared of Mr. Lincoln's belongings and the bust would be damaged.

As I was escorted down the halls I saw that the mirrors had been veiled and the red damask curtains at every window had been draped in black. We walked by the East Room, where Mr. Lincoln's catafalque was being prepared for the thousands of mourners who would soon pass by to honor him. I paused for a moment to watch as the central chandelier was removed from the ceiling to make room for the bier's great height while black crepe was hung on the other two chandeliers.

Having asked leave to pay my respects to Mr. Lincoln, I stood for a while by his casket. Sunlight spilled through the windows and touched the coffin—it was studded with silver nails that glittered like stars. The light on the nails hurt my eyes, and I realized that I was weeping.

My escort, a soldier of much patience, sympathetically offered me his arm, and we continued on towards Mr. Lincoln's office. On Friday, the soldier told me, the casket will be placed on the funeral train for the slow journey to Springfield, Illinois, where Mr. Lincoln will be buried. He mentioned, too, that the train will carry Willie's small casket, for the child will be placed at the feet of his father.

When we entered Mr. Lincoln's office I looked over at his desk where he had often sat reading while I sat with my clay. Memories warmed my heart. I remembered his eyes, his beautifully gentle eyes. I remembered how he watched Tad with pride whenever he darted about the room like a tiny bolt of lightning. I remembered how he gazed with love at his wife's sweet face whenever she bustled into the room with a tray of food. And I remembered how he looked upon me with fatherly kindness.

The soldier helped me place my tools and clay in a box and then left to find a cart to carry out the sculpture. While he was gone I unwrapped the towel—it was still damp— from around the bust and looked at the likeness I had made of Mr. Lincoln's face.

I believe, Regina, that I captured Mr. Lincoln's expression of unfathomable Sadness. There was no skill involved; my hands merely obeyed my heart's recognition of his Two Faces of Sorrow.

Standing by the window, the same window that had brought about one of those faces, I gazed over the lawns. This morning the sun gleamed like gold and the grasses glistened green from the recent rains.

Then, Regina, I looked with my heart instead of my eyes. And with my heart's vision I could see Mr. Lincoln crossing the lawns, his giant hand holding the small hand of his son. And I could see that Mr. Lincoln's dear, dear face had finally lost its Sadness.

Friday, April 21

Early this morning my family, Senator Ross, and I joined thousands of mourners at the railroad station to see Mr. Lincoln's funeral train depart. We watched as his casket and his son's much smaller casket were placed on the train. We then looked about for Mrs. Lincoln to offer our condolences but learned that grief has forced her into her sickbed.

Near me, on the edge of the platform, a group of gentlemen waited to board the train. Among them stood Senator Lyman Trumbull. Perhaps you'll remember him as my benefactor, Regina, for it was he who asked Mr. Lincoln's permission for me to sculpt him—that memorable day now seems years, rather than months, ago. I lifted my hand in greeting, but Senator Trumbull did not notice. No doubt his eyes were blurred by his sorrow, for he twice removed and wiped his spectacles before stepping up onto the train. He and many others will accompany Mr. Lincoln to Illinois.

Surrounding me on the platform were other mourners, each of us bidding a silent farewell to Mr. Lincoln. None of us wore a hat. We, the ladies, held our bonnets while they, the gentlemen, bared their heads in respect. We stood in quiet, our eyes turned towards the train as though we believed that Mr. Lincoln would miraculously appear at the door and step down amongst us, but that miracle failed to happen. Silence hung like a shroud upon all our hearts, and we denied ourselves the liberty of speaking or even breathing. All at once the silence was broken by the clanging of the engine's bells, which knelled like death bells as the doors slid shut and the train slowly pulled away towards other cities where other mourners are waiting.

When my family and I arrived home we were greeted by an amazing sight. Outside our house stood a long line of people, all of them waiting for me. It seems, dear friend, that a newspaper article had been written about my sessions with Mr. Lincoln.

Ma asked me to keep the crowd outside while she hurriedly swept the parlor, and then in they came, one by one—perhaps a hundred or more men, women, and children who wished to look upon the face of Mr. Lincoln. I sat near the bust and watched the expressions change on my visitors' faces when first they saw the sculpture. "Such sad eyes," some said with tears in their own eyes. "Such kindness in his mouth," others said. Still others said, "Such wisdom on his brow." Their comments gladdened my heart, for they recognized what I had recognized in the actual face of Mr. Lincoln—his sadness, his kindness, and his wisdom.

Long after night had fallen, the curious knocked on our door. Perhaps my sculpture has a purpose, Regina, for it seems to comfort those who refuse to forget Mr. Lincoln.

Monday, April 24
How wonderful that Michael has returned safely to your side! And how marvelous that you have decided on November for

your wedding. I will arrive in Missouri by early October so that we shall have time to sew our gowns. I look forward to meeting your betrothed and seeing you again, dear friend, after all these years of separation.

What exciting news that you and Michael shall live in New York City! We must visit each other often. And how splendid that Michael himself will design your house! If ever I should marry I will hire your husband as my architect.

This letter must be brief, for I hear Ma in the kitchen and I want to help her prepare breakfast. I am sorely worried about her, Regina, for she barely touches her food and her face has grown thin and pale. For days now, she has refused to leave the house in case Bob should suddenly appear, and I doubt she sleeps at night as she listens for his step at our door. Pa has explained that it may be weeks or even months before we see Bob, but Ma imagines that every footfall belongs to my brother.

Thursday, April 27

This morning when I arrived at the Post Office I learned that I am no longer employed—the clerk I replaced more than two years ago has returned safely from the War and is in need of his position. Although I will miss the camaraderie of my fellow workers, my family won't suffer overmuch, for I receive handsome commissions for sculpting head portraits.

As I walked home from the Post Office, small boys peddling newspapers called out the headline—"John Wilkes Booth Shot to Death in Virginia!" I'm sure your newspaper reported the story of Booth's mad dash yesterday from the burning barn and the shots that wounded him and his confession before his death, but did your newspaper mention that his journals have been found and that his own words clearly detail his plot?

Surely he was an evil man and it is far better that he no longer walks in this world.

On my arrival home I found my mother sobbing on her bed, for she fears my brother is dead. There have been premonitions of Bob's death, she believes—in the design that tea leaves made in her cup and in the winds that moaned around our house. She refuses to listen to Pa's explanations that Bob might be fighting in the skirmishes that are continuing down South, or that he might be walking home from a great distance. Ma refuses to listen to any explanation except that he is dead.

Supper was a sombre meal. Mary and I tried to distract Ma by talking of fashions and music, but she would not be drawn into frivolous conversation. Her food untasted, she retired to the parlor and sat with her knitting on her lap. Not once did she pick up her needles; instead, she stared at the cold hearth, and though she shivered, she refused to let Pa light a fire. As night crept into our parlor, Ma insisted that the lamps remain dimmed. No one spoke a word because she asked that we sit in quiet so as not to interrupt her prayers. None of us knew how to comfort her, so we sat near her in silence until she rose, wordlessly, and walked slowly up the stairs.

Ma is finally asleep, but her head tosses on her pillow and we know her dreams are troubled. Oh, Regina, surely my brother is alive, and yet—where is he?

Friday, May 5

Tonight during supper we heard loud knocking. Somewhat annoyed by the interruption to our meal, Pa answered the door. A moment later we heard him murmur, "Bob ..." and Mary and I took flight from our chairs.

My brother stood in the doorway, or rather he leaned

against the frame of the door as though he possessed no strength to stand on his own. He was taller than us all—his head nearly reached the top of the door—but he carried so little flesh on his bones that he resembled a scarecrow that had lost its hay to the wind. His hair was still red, but it was matted and dirty and fell to his shoulders in tangles. Dark shadows hung like black half-moons beneath his blue eyes, and his lips were puffy and cracked and speckled with bits of blood. His uniform hung in strips over his chest and legs and arms—indeed, the rags lent him more of that scarecrowish appearance. Both his feet were shoeless and yet he looked as if he wore brown stockings. I realized with horror that his feet were caked with aged blood. One of his hands had freshly bled, for the filthy rag about his wound was red and wet.

Except for the blue eyes and red hair that he inherited from Ma, I wouldn't have recognized that living scarecrow as my brother, but then he smiled and I remembered all at once my brother's endearing, crooked smile.

Ma came behind us more slowly as though she doubted that Bob was home. Seeing the scarecrow in the doorway caused her to pause, and she stared at my brother as if he were a mirage. And then a beautiful smile touched her gentle face and she lifted her arms towards him. Slowly Bob stepped from the shadows towards Ma, and then, crying out like a frightened child, he rushed into her arms.

Such celebrating at my house has never been seen. After rounds and rounds of hugs and kisses, Pa filled the tub for Bob, and soon he came downstairs clean and warm in his old robe (it was much too short). Pa made Bob comfortable in his rocker, and while he lit the fire in the hearth, my sister dressed Bob's wounded hand and feet. By then Ma and I had prepared a tray of stew and hot bread. My brother ate hungrily, at the same time asking news of ourselves. And yet, Regina, when we asked him news of his years away he would only answer, "Tomorrow. I'll tell you tomorrow."

Peaceful sleep is upon my family now, but sleep escapes me. I am much too excited to close my eyes, for I am convinced that Bob's safe arrival home is a Sign—a Sign that our Nation will now know Peace. Everlasting Peace.

Friday, June 9

It was thoughtful of you to welcome my brother home. He intends to answer your letter soon, but don't be surprised by the brevity of his message. Bob speaks nothing of himself. Every time we ask him of his years during the War he answers, "Tomorrow. I'll tell you tomorrow." My family now understands that tomorrow will never come.

Regina, is your betrothed having difficulty adjusting to civil-ian life? My brother looks healthy again, but his spirit must be damaged. Daily he invents excuses to stay at home. At first he wished to stay home until his hand healed, but Ma's slimy cheese quickly cured that wound. Next he complained of weariness, but he sleeps away the hours of each day.

Ma urges us to be patient with Bob, but Pa is concerned by his strange behavior—for example, last week Pa asked Bob to help him carry some maps to his office. Upon their arrival home, perspiration spotted my brother's face even though the day was unseasonably cool. Pa told us later that Bob acted nervous throughout their walk—made nervous by the close passage of carriages and horses, the shoppers who crowded the pavement, the noise and color and movement of our busy city. Since that one outing, Bob has refused to step outside the house.

1 8 6 5

We have noticed, too, his dread of the dark. Before dusk has even settled, he lights the fire in the hearth and brightens every lamp in the house. And when he retires, he sleeps with a lighted lamp by his bed.

Please write to me at once, Regina, and quiet my worries.

Wednesday, June 28

Earlier tonight, Ma and Pa dined with friends and Mary went shopping for yarn, so my brother and I were home alone. He sat at the kitchen table eating, of course, while I pasted labels on jars of berry preserves that Ma had put up this afternoon. In between mouthfuls of apple pie, Bob spoke about our childhood homes in Missouri and Arkansas. My brother seemed almost wistful as he recalled our friends there and the beauty of the wind-swept fields and rolling hills.

After I had finished marking the labels, Bob offered to help me carry the jars down the cellar steps to the pantry shelves. As I mentioned in my previous letter, he fears darkness, so his offer surprised me—the cellar is quite dark (only a bit of light spills down the steps from the kitchen).

As we stacked the jars we heard footsteps above and then Mary's voice, but before we could call out to her the cellar door slammed shut. In the very moment when the cellar became pitch black, I heard the crash of breaking glass and then a piercing, terrifying scream. At once the door opened and light fled down the steps to reveal my brother crouching on the floor. His arms were wrapped around his head and his face was pressed against his knees as his screams changed into low moans of pain.

At first I thought the shattered jars had cut him, but there was no sign of blood. Mary rushed down the steps, and I warned her with a quick shake of my head not to speak, for I knew somehow that Bob was beyond questioning. Between us we coaxed him upstairs and into the parlor, where we laid him gently on the sofa. He shivered violently in spite of the blankets wrapped around him. Mary added wood to the fire, and after a while the intense heat overcame him and his eyes closed.

My parents returned while Bob slept. Mary and I told them what had happened, and then we all sat near him and waited for him to awaken. A long hour passed before he awoke. At first he seemed dazed by our presence; then realization must have dawned on him, for he looked at each of us in turn before saying, "You have asked me about my years away. Perhaps I should tell you now."

Oh, Regina, he told us about the War. He told us what we had guessed about his times of hunger and cold and illness, and he told of his fear during battles and the loneliness that engulfed him at times. And then he told us of one particular night.

Towards the end of the War Bob had lived for months in one of those horrible trenches that surrounded Petersburg. I had always imagined those deep holes as graves, and from my brother's description my imagination proved accurate. The trenches were merciless places—hot by day, cold by night, alive with crawling rats and lice, and foul with vomit and human waste.

One night, mere days before the Confederates retreated to escape General Grant's army, Bob and his fellow soldiers were crowded together in a deep trench. All day they had been blasted by Union artillery while heavy rains fell, and by nightfall their trench was knee-deep with water. And yet, exhausted beyond reason, they slept. Dear friend, those rains had saturated the ground and the walls became so sodden that they caved in, sending an avalanche of mud and stone down on the sleeping men. Bob found himself trapped from his neck down in the sea of mud, an inch or so of mud covering his face. For several minutes he gasped for air, choking and gagging on the dirt filling his mouth and nose, while above him he heard the shouts of men and the scraping sounds of shovels. Bob struggled to push his face clear of the drowning mud—but that is all he remembers, for he lost consciousness. When he awoke, he was lying above the ground—but he had been mistaken for dead. Piled on top of my brother and all around him were dead soldiers who had suffocated beneath the mud.

Since his ordeal, my brother cannot tolerate dark places, for the darkness reminds him of that trench. Nor can he tolerate crowds, for he is reminded of that terrible awakening when he found himself crushed under the bodies of dead friends.

After telling us of these horrors, my brother seems more at peace with himself. Perhaps he has released some of the memories haunting him.

A short while ago I remembered the jar of preserves that Bob had broken and realized that ants would swarm into our cellar by morning. The house was dark and quiet, and so I tiptoed downstairs. I was startled to find the lamp lit in the kitchen, but then I noticed that the door to the cellar was open. Peering downstairs I saw Bob sweeping up the broken glass. Somehow, Regina, my brother had found the courage to return to that dark cellar. I pray God that he finds added courage to venture back into the world.

P.S.—How wonderful that Michael has returned to you healthy and happy! I wish Bob could have come home without his memories of War.

Wednesday, July 5

Every morning, before the city of Washington awakes, Pa and Bob go for a long walk. My brother gains strength from those walks, for he always returns smiling his wonderful crooked smile. And every afternoon, when Pa is home from work, he teaches Bob the craft of surveying and mapmaking. My brother spends most of his other hours practicing with the mapping tools—he no longer sleeps his hours away.

Regina, since that terrible night in the cellar my brother has not suffered a similar episode. True, at times he has terrible dreams, but they are becoming less frequent and less frightening. Perhaps the most telling sign that Bob is healing is that he doesn't flee upstairs whenever someone knocks at the door.

It is well that my brother doesn't mind company, for we receive many visitors. On most days strangers and friends alike drop by to look at the bust of Mr. Lincoln. Senator Trumbull has visited several times, each time accompanied by a different group of senators. General Ulysses S. Grant has even stopped by! Pleased by my work, he has requested that I sculpt a portrait of his head.

This morning Senator Ross returned from Kansas, where he was visiting his wife and children. He was happy to see Bob after all these years and told us that he will begin his search for a house at once, so that Bob can reclaim his old bedroom (Bob has been sleeping on a cot in the kitchen).

It is because of Senator Ross that I have exciting news about myself. At supper tonight he proved that his kind remarks about the bust were sincere, for he suggested that I enter the contest that has ignited the interest of every sculptor in America—the contest to win a government commission to sculpt a life-size statue of Mr. Lincoln that will stand in a place of honor in the

Rotunda of the Capitol building!

The senator's suggestion startled me so much that I spilled gravy on our lace tablecloth, but Ma took no notice. She clapped her hands together and urged me to enter the contest. Believing that Senator Ross was teasing me, I laughed and reminded him that a woman has never received a commission from our government and that I am an unknown sculptress. Senator Ross smiled back at me and reminded me that I am the last sculptor that Mr. Lincoln sat for. Oh, Regina, I decided at once to enter!

After supper Senator Ross and I sat at the kitchen table for nearly two hours, and with his patient assistance I composed a letter that explained how Senator Trumbull had introduced me to Mr. Lincoln and told of our sessions together. I took care to use simple words to express my keen desire to be chosen for the commission to sculpt the statue of Mr. Lincoln.

Once I had sealed the letter I decided to mail it immediately, before my courage deserted me, and this is where I come to the most exciting news of all—as I was leaving the house Bob offered to walk with me to the Post Office! Even though the streets were crowded and the darkness of night had fallen, he wanted to escort me there himself! And so I took my brother's arm and we walked out into the night.

Tuesday, August 15

I have no desire to write this letter, but I must. Oh, Regina, Ma will not allow my family to attend your wedding! Washington's newspapers publish colorful stories of those awful James brothers, and Ma's imagination adds more color. Until they are jailed, she refuses to step foot on a westbound train, and she won't hear of my traveling alone. I am sorry, Regina, but neither Pa nor I could convince my mother otherwise.

Dear friend, can you find it in your heart to forgive our absence on your wedding day?

Friday, September 1

Your gracious letter lifted my spirits. Until you reminded me, I had quite forgotten that your aunt once forbade you to travel by train—back then and now, those terrible outlaws have caused my mother and your aunt much fear. How I wish Frank and Jesse James would be captured and jailed!

You must promise to write a long letter describing every moment of your wedding day, and you must send me your addresses from each country you visit. How exciting that Michael wants to lengthen your wedding trip in Europe—his notion of studying European architecture is intriguing. Roaming through the aged cities of England and the Continent for two long years will bring you and Michael adventures that others only dream about! Perhaps through your letters I, too, will discover the wonders of London and Paris and Rome and Vienna.

Sunday, September 24

As always, your thoughtful birthday gift has touched my heart. I received another gift today, a quite unexpected one from someone I once loved—my poet, John Rollin Ridge.

John sent me a packet of letters he has been writing since 1861—dozens and dozens of letters that he never posted. His first letter is dated June 29, the very day my train pulled away from Fort Smith.

In a letter written last month, John explained that because I was a child and he was more than twenty years my senior he thought it proper to wait until the occasion of my eighteenth birthday to mail me the packet. After reading the letters I can understand why, for each one closes with a profession of his love.

John also enclosed a foil-wrapped gift in the packet—a book of his own poetry! Between two of its pages I found a piece of white paper, upon which was written an offer of eternal love. Regina, my sweet Poet wishes to marry me. Thrice I read his proposal before noticing that the verses printed on those two pages, 5 and 6, is the poem "How Do I Love Thee," the very one he wrote for me when I was just a child.

Oh, Regina, I once dreamed of receiving letters from my Poet, letters just like these, but now I read them with a confused heart. My confusion is because of his cousin, Boudy. It is he whom I love, and yet Boudy hasn't come courting as I believed he would, now that War has ended. How should I answer John's proposal? Should I tell him his declaration of love has come too late? Or has it? I loved John once—perhaps I could look upon him again with tender eyes. Dear friend, whatever shall I do?

Wednesday, November 1

On your wedding day I will imagine myself standing in the Academy's old chapel listening and rejoicing as you and Michael speak your vows and are joined forever as husband and wife.

I was uncertain what to send as my wedding gift, so I decided on two gifts. The silver teaspoons are for both you and Michael. They were crafted by a renowned silversmith from the Maryland city of Annapolis. The other gift is a special one for you, dear friend. I asked the silversmith to design a locket in the shape of a rose, for you have always reminded me of that fragile flower. Open the locket, Regina, and you shall find your name and the name of your betrothed engraved within.

Ma and Pa, Mary and Bob and I send you and Michael our fondest wishes for a long life of infinite joy.

P.S.—I have answered John's letter of proposal. It was difficult to find the words to reject his love without wounding his gentle heart, but how could I marry a man whom I have come to look upon as a beloved brother?

Sunday, Christmas Eve

My family received a long letter from your aunt—twenty pages in all! She wrote about your wedding in such detail that I felt as though I had been in attendance. Your aunt described you as a "heavenly angel floating down the aisle in a cloud of silk and lace." How pleased I am to learn that you took my suggestion to bead your veil with seed pearls. Your aunt also wrote glowingly about Michael—how tall he stood, how handsome was his face, how proud he looked. She described the wedding luncheon (and included several recipes for Ma) and sent me your address in London. London! Write soon and describe every inch of that aged city.

This has been a peaceful Christmas. My brother is so much improved that he can go out into the streets without anxiety. In truth, Bob dislikes the rushing traffic and the noise and crowds of Washington, but at least his displeasure is not based on fear. His surveying skills are keen now, and soon he will apply for a position as a surveyor or mapmaker. I doubt he will look for work in Washington, though, for he prefers green fields to paved roads.

Ma, Pa, and Mary are faring well in health and spirit. Of late, my sister has been courted by an interesting gentleman named Major Perry Fuller, a widower with four small daughters.

Regina, did I mention in a previous letter that I still stop by the Post Office to sing for the wounded? Sadly, there are still soldiers housed there, for some are too injured or too weak to return to their homes, while others have no homes to return to. The number of patients decreases daily, but as long as one soldier remains there I shall sing willingly.

This afternoon when I arrived at the hospital I was greeted by Mrs. Wooten. (Does she ever go home?) Beside her desk sat a girl, much our own age. She was pretty, with curls the color of ripe strawberries that tumbled from under her bonnet and framed her heart-shaped face. I could tell by her downcast eyes and the sickly color of her complexion that she had glimpsed the horrors of the rooms beyond.

Mrs. Wooten introduced her to me as Miss Bridget Mulqueen. When she took my hand and raised her face up, I was struck by the clearness and goodness shining in her brown eyes. Before we could speak, though, a voice sang out from behind the door—the heaven-sent voice of James Kilmar.

At once I dashed through the door, and the moment James finished his song I hugged him warmly. My behavior was forward, I know, but I have come to regard him as my own brother and could scarcely conceal my joy at seeing him again. For a long while we sang Christmas carols, and the blending of our two voices clearly pleased the soldiers. Afterwards, after we bade the men Happy Christmas, we walked arm in arm through the door to Mrs. Wooten's desk.

There I was given another surprise—Bridget and James are betrothed! They intend to marry after he completes his training at the music conservatory. Tonight my family will meet Bridget, for she, James, and Mrs. Kilmar will soon arrive to share our Christmas goose.

The merriest of holidays to you, dear Regina, and to your dear husband, Michael.

1866

Tuesday, January 9

My dear friend Regina,

I read your descriptions of Buckingham Palace and West-minster Abbey a thousand times over, and impatiently I await your next letter.

In answer to your questions about the contest, the winning sculptor has not yet been named. The selection will take time, for the House of Representatives and the Senate must both approve the winner. Today I discovered that my teacher, Mr. Mills, has entered his application—surely he will win, for the angel he cast for the crown of the Capitol's dome has been applauded. If by some chance the commission is awarded to a woman, I am certain that talented sculptress from Maine, Miss Harriet Hosmer, will be chosen. My entry will be overlooked, I do not doubt.

Major Perry Fuller is still courting my sister. You would like him, Regina, for he is utterly charming. Pa learned that his reputation as a businessman is sterling—indeed, he is quite wealthy, owning three magnificent homes (one in Lawrenceville, Kansas, one in New York City, and one here in Washington). Three years ago his wife passed on and since then he has been both father and mother to his daughters (such darling girls, aged three, five, seven, and nine). All four resemble their father, for they inherited his tar-black hair and his laughing blue eyes. My sister has been courted by men even wealthier and even more handsome than Major Fuller, but he is different from her other beaux in that he possesses a rare gift: Laughter. Mary confided that his laughter lightens her heart whenever she hears it, which is often, for he is a man who finds pleasure in simple things—a child at play, a song, a starlit sky, a walk by the river.

Saturday, March 24

There is much—so very much—to write about. As you know, I sculpt head portraits in clay, which betters my skills as a sculptor while helping my parents financially. This morning I was working in the parlor on the head of a matron of society, Mrs. Hubert Hutchinson, when there came rapid knocking at our door. I was hardly presentable, for I was frocked in my oldest dress with my hair tied back with a strip of cloth and wet clay smearing my face and hands, but I answered the front door nonetheless.

On the step sat a gilded cage, within which a snow-white dove cooed prettily. Puzzled, I pushed my finger through the wire and stroked the bird's soft, feathered head. I noticed, then, someone standing in the shadow of the door, and believing him to be the delivery boy, I turned with a smile. Oh, Regina, he was no boy—it was Boudy. My Boudy!

He stood there in the shadows, his hat in his hand with a smile embracing his face, and my heart danced with ecstasy. He is still handsome, despite the passage of time, for he is all of thirty years now. His black hair still waves about his face in that wild, wind-swept way I always cherished, and his eyes, though lined from the sun, still glow when he speaks. And his voice! Oh, Regina, his voice! I had forgotten how his voice makes my heart sing.

And then I remembered my untidy appearance and I melted into the earth. So many times I've dreamt of meeting him again and in those dreams I always pictured myself in a flowered gown, with roses in my hair and perfume scenting my wrists, but there I stood in my stained dress with a rag dangling from my hair and smelling of wet clay.

I took his hands, but he—oh, Regina, how can I tell you this, but I must—he caught me up in his arms and kissed my mouth! There! I have admitted it. To my shame, I will never forget that moment.

Behind me, Mrs. Hutchinson gasped. After pulling myself away from Boudy's embrace I ushered him into the hall and introduced them. Mrs. Hutchinson bristled about the interruption, and so although it was difficult to concentrate on my work, I returned to sculpting the lady's head. Boudy sat in the corner watching me, and whenever I glanced at him I colored from the amusement in his eyes.

My mother came into the parlor and greeted Boudy warmly, insisting that he join her and Bob in the kitchen for tea. Before she left the room she whispered to me, "I'll distract him while you change into your taffeta gown." Ma is such a dear!

As soon as I could hurry Mrs. Hutchinson out the door, I fled upstairs and slipped into my prettiest dress and brushed the clay from my hair. I wished roses were in bloom, but as they are not, I pinched my cheeks until they reddened like roses before I ran down the steps. I paused outside the kitchen, struggling to catch my breath, and then walked slowly through the door. When Boudy saw me, the look in his eyes as he stood up bespoke his approval.

Pa and Mary arrived soon after that, and for a long while we reminisced about our old home in Fort Smith, plaguing Boudy with endless questions about neighbors and friends we had known.

Before supper Ma suggested that I take Boudy for a walk about the city—bless my mother's romantic heart—and so at long last I was alone with him, my arm on his, as we strolled the streets of Washington. I have no idea what we spoke about or if we even spoke, but I remembered as we turned down Pennsylvania Avenue that I had often dreamt of strolling with Boudy down that very street. Finally, finally, Regina, my dream had come true.

Supper was a noisy occasion. Senator Ross took an instant liking to Boudy and asked him much about his role in restoring relations between our government and the Cherokee Indians. Then, during a pause in the conversation, Senator Ross happened to mention my entry in the contest to sculpt Mr. Lincoln's statue.

Regina, I will never forget the extraordinary change that came over Boudy's face at the mere mention of Mr. Lincoln. His eyes narrowed as though with pain, and his mouth tightened and hardened. Even his voice changed to a voice laced with bitterness when he said, "I hope you lose."

I could not believe what I had heard. Mutely I listened as he began to speak about Mr. Lincoln and the Union with such hatred that his wrath washed over us like a wave of fetid water. I knew that my parents, Mary, and Senator Ross were offended, and I could see that my brother, the onetime Confederate soldier, was embarrassed. All the magic of the afternoon and the merriment of the evening vanished like a puff of smoke in the wind.

Boudy is staying at a hotel on Pennsylvania Avenue. Before he bade us good night he pulled me aside and kissed me again, but this time his kiss tasted bitter. As he buttoned his coat I noticed the caged dove sitting on the hallway floor. In the excitement I had forgotten to thank him and so I did, but in an irritable voice he told me that the gift was not his to give, that he had only delivered it.

After the door had closed behind him I knelt down by the cage. The bird fluttered his snowy feathers as I pulled off a card tied to the roof of the cage. On the card my Dear Poet, John

Rollin Ridge, had written, "Little Vinnie, you always reminded me of this serene bird." Bending over the cage, I wept.

Pa mistook my tears. He thought my grief was caused by Boudy's departure for the night, but in truth I wept because I wished that Boudy was John and that John was Boudy—oh, how confused I must sound, Regina! I wept because I wished I could take parts of each man, the gentleness of John and the strength of Boudy, and shape those parts into a whole man I could entrust my heart to forever.

Thursday, April 5

This evening Boudy and I dined at the Willard Hotel with my sister and her gentleman friend, Major Perry Fuller. The evening should have been romantic. Candlelight cast rainbows through our crystal wine glasses and shimmered over the silver platters while the music of violins softened the voices of other diners. Mary and I wore our most elegant gowns, mine of ivory satin and lace, and hers of green silk (my sister looked beautiful, as always), and Boudy and Major Fuller were handsome in their suits of black. But romance was vanquished, for the conversation centered around the War.

Until this evening I hadn't known that Major Fuller had distinguished himself on fields of battle. And yet, though Boudy raged against Northern generals and criticized the Union's victory, Major Fuller acted the perfect gentleman. Indeed, he tried to soothe Boudy's temper with jovial humor, but Boudy responded to the Major's witticisms with acerbic remarks. By the time the dessert cart was brought to our table, I longed to escape to my attic room where I could cry myself to sleep.

Boudy has been here in Washington for less than two weeks, and yet I feel as though I have labored through two long years with him. His bitterness drags down my heart and shadows my soul with sadness. I cannot tolerate his ill temper.

When I am alone, Regina, I cry constantly, my tears refusing to dry up. I long to bring back the last five years, when I refused gentleman callers and preferred instead to sit in my attic room and dream about Boudy. The man I dreamt about has his heart locked in an iron cage.

He is leaving for Arkansas tomorrow. When I bid him farewell it will be as an old friend, not as his sweetheart.

P.S.—Now it is Friday—I have unsealed the envelope to add this postscript. Boudy stopped by this morning to say his farewells. I pretended his leaving saddened me, for his heart is already too tainted to bear the bitterness of the truth—that I was relieved to say good-bye.

My brother left with Boudy on the noon train to Arkansas. (Surely the long train journey will seem shorter in the company of an old friend.) They will travel together to Fort Smith, where Bob is certain to find employment as a surveyor.

Before my brother left I gave him a sketch I had drawn of myself with the dove on my shoulder (I have named my dove "Poet," which should please John). Bob promised to deliver the drawing to John.

Ma was beside herself with sorrow at Bob's sudden leave-taking, but she realizes, as we all do, that he is seeking a more peaceful life away from the paved streets of Washington—he will find that peace surrounded by mountains and fields of wild grasses.

Oh, Regina, I pray that Boudy finds his own source of peace, for his heart is still at War with our Nation.

Wednesday, June 6

I received your long letter and thrilled to your descriptions of

Paris and the French countryside. Your colorful words painted a picture in my mind—I could visualize the stonework of those ancient cathedrals, the grapes dotting the vineyards, the flowers climbing over the village roofs. How I wish you could gather the blossoms that cling to those cottages and bring home the bouquet, so that I, too, could smell the perfume of French flowers. How magnificent it must be to see such beauty with your own eyes.

This letter is a happy one. My darling sister is betrothed to that splendid gentleman, Major Perry Fuller. Ma is ecstatic, for she recognizes in Major Fuller the same gentle goodness of my pa—indeed, Mary recognized their resemblance the moment they first met. Pa is pleased, for he respects Major Fuller as both an honorable man and an astute businessman who can provide my sister with a life of luxury.

And I, Regina, am overjoyed, for I am fond of Major Fuller. He never fails to be serious when a serious nature is needed, and yet if the moment calls for laughter he can draw a smile from anyone. After all those dark years of War, our Nation needs men who still know how to laugh.

Mary and Major Fuller plan to wed on Christmas Eve—I shall make head portraits of them both as my wedding gift.

P.S.—In answer to your question about the contest—no one has been chosen yet. How kind you are to encourage me, but I'm afraid your hope far outweighs my own of being selected.

Monday, July 30

Three days ago Senator Lyman Trumbull called on my parents and me. We determined at once that he was excited about something, but we had no idea of the cause. Having refused a glass of sherry, he took my hand, bowed, and said, "Vinnie, yesterday the House of Representatives passed a Resolution to contract you to sculpt the statue of Mr. Lincoln."

I gasped, Regina, not trusting my ears.

Still holding my hand, Senator Trumbull told me that this morning the Resolution was brought from the House to the floor of the Senate Chamber for approval or denial. The debate was long and savage, for some of the senators were enraged that I, an inexperienced sculptress, should be awarded $10,000 while other, more renowned sculptors were passed over. Senator Trumbull said that tempers flared so violently at times that one of his colleagues remarked, "It is no ordinary girl who can shake and agitate this chamber to its very center." I did have my supporters, such as Senator Nesmith of Oregon, who kindly described me as a sculptress with "intuitive genius" (how good he was to say that!). Still holding my hand in his, Senator Trumbull assured me that twenty-two other senators agreed with Senator Nesmith—a vote was taken and the majority voted to grant me the commission!

His happy news imparted, Senator Trumbull released my hand. Numb with disbelief, I stared at him and wondered if I walked in a dream. But it was no dream. I have been chosen to sculpt the statue of Abraham Lincoln! My heart's fondest desire—to sculpt Mr. Lincoln—has come true. Again.

Thursday, August 30

Three hours ago I met with the Interior Secretary, Mr. James Harlan, who presented me with a contract that commits me to sculpt, in plaster, a life-size statue of Mr. Lincoln.

The contract says that when the plaster statue is completed it must be inspected by the Interior Secretary. If it is approved by him, I will be given the first payment of $5,000. I must then carve a duplicate of that plaster statue in marble, and if that second statue is approved by our government, I will be given a second payment of $5,000.

I read the document twice and then picked up a pen and signed my name—my signature looked scratched, like the unpracticed penmanship of a child, and I realized that I was shaking violently.

Mr. Harlan graciously escorted me to a sculpting studio in the basement of the Capitol building—Studio A. It is a large enough room, though drab and dirty and lacking any furniture except a broken chair and a long table. Slowly I walked around the room, not minding the peeling paint or the soiled floor, for there was one redeeming feature—a window wide enough for the sun to drench the room with brightness.

Because I shan't be given any money until the plaster statue is finished and approved, I must furnish the studio with my own money. I must therefore accept more commissions for head portraits until I can afford the tools and plaster I will need. Until then, my studio must remain empty of my presence.

P.S.—Do you remember my constant dreams in which I carved rocks into statues of the Indian children I loved? How far I have traveled since those childhood dreams!

Saturday, September 15
Your last letter distressed me greatly—I hasten to lessen your worries about my reputation. Yes, I have read Mrs. Jane Swisshelm's newspaper articles about me, although I wish I hadn't. I pretend in public that I don't care what she writes, but in private I care very much. I was shocked to hear that your newspapers in Europe have printed her slanderous remarks about me—it is bad enough that her articles are printed in every large city of our

Nation. I'm not sure why she writes such malignant, vulgar, and unprovoked things about me, but there is one possible cause for her abuse. I have heard that she had hoped that her close friend, the sculptress Miss Harriet Hosmer, would be granted the commission in my place.

Supposedly, Regina, Mrs. Swisshelm has only seen me once, and then from a distance, and yet she describes me in such minute detail that I feel like an insect under the magnifying glass of a scientist. Her accusation that I used feminine charms to win the sculpting commission offends me, for I did not lobby the senators to win their votes. Mrs. Swisshelm may call my dresses fine if she so wishes, but how cruel of her to describe my jewelry as gaudy (my necklaces and earrings were crafted by Indian artisans). Regina, has Mrs. Swisshelm reported my name as "Minnie" in her column in your newspaper? Often she addresses me as such in pieces she writes for Washington's newspapers.

Perhaps I shouldn't care what Mrs. Swisshelm says, but her words wound my heart. Her blows aim higher than my profession as a sculptress, for she aims at my character and my life.

Unfortunately, Mrs. Swisshelm isn't my only enemy. The lady journalist from Connecticut, Mrs. Ann Stephens, is even more determined to turn the Nation against me with her poisonous pen. She doesn't stop there, however, for she also appears at large gatherings to denounce me as a fake and a pretender. Senator Ross told me that during her recent visit to Washington she stopped by the Capitol to urge Congress to close my studio before I even begin the sculpture.

In answer to your second question, Regina, I have not earned enough money to open my studio. I have purchased some of the equipment I will need, such as the iron rods for the armatures (rods that support the statue's weight), but I still need to buy tools and hundreds of bags of plaster. Fortunately I sculpt head portraits with great speed, so I can accept a new commission each week. At this time I am finishing a bust of the Editor of the *New York Tribune* newspaper, Mr. Horace Greeley. Ironically, that is one of the newspapers Mrs. Swisshelm writes for, and I've heard that she flew into a rage when she learned I was sculpting Mr. Greeley.

Until I can open my studio, I work at my desk here at home. In the peace of my attic room I refuse to think of those vindictive women while I draw sketches of the statue. When I stop by the studio, though, to paint the walls or scrub the floor, their cruel falsehoods drift into my mind. Regina, I intend to prove those women wrong—I will prove that Congress chose me because of my skills as a sculptress and not because I wear Indian jewelry and long curls!

Monday, September 24
My birthday has passed happily, for I dined tonight with Mary and her betrothed, Major Fuller, and my parents at a quaint restaurant on New York Avenue. Afterwards we attended a marvelous concert of American music, where I ran into a gentleman who once called on me with persistence. He invited me to sup with him tomorrow at the Willard, and I accepted gladly. No longer will I deny myself the company of gentlemen, for Boudy has stepped out of my heart.

I received your thoughtful remembrance yesterday. Never have I owned a lovelier necklace! I wore it tonight and received many compliments. The amber matches the color of my eyes perfectly, Ma says.

And thank you, dear friend, for your marvelous description

and sketches of Rome. How I enjoyed reading about your walks along its winding streets. How wonderful to wander about a city where the citizens speak a tongue so foreign, and yet so musical, to your ears. Regina, were you exaggerating, or do hundreds of cats truly slink about the ancient Roman Amphitheatre?

Of particular interest to me were your fascinating remarks about the American artists in the old quarter of Rome—what eccentric behavior some of them employ! Do you realize, Regina, that if my plaster statue is approved by our government, I will be given the first half of the money—I would be wealthy! Then I, too, could travel to Rome and live in the artists' colony. After all, I would need to visit the marble quarries of Carrara, Italy, to select the purest, whitest piece of stone, so that my plaster statue could be carved in marble—it has become my belief that the purity of the marble determines the beauty of a finished sculpture.

Of course my plaster statue might be judged a failure by the Interior Secretary, and if so, months and months of hard work will be wasted. In the unhappy event that my statue should fail the inspection, I will visit Rome by reading your letters once again.

Monday, October 8

I still haven't enough money to purchase the bags of plaster or the furnishings for my studio, although I have acquired many of the tools. Unable to work there as yet, I sit at my attic windows each day and plan the steps I will take when I can finally begin sculpting.

My approach will be unusual. First I will sculpt the form of the statue without drapings. Once the figure is completed I will invite Mr. Lincoln's former doctors to examine the statue to judge if the anatomical measurements are accurate. Ma was flabbergasted when I told her that I intend to sculpt a naked Mr. Lincoln. After Pa aided me in my explanation, Ma came to understand that my approach will render a true-to-life figure of Mr. Lincoln. She made me promise, though, to ban ladies from my studio until Mr. Lincoln is properly attired.

Second, I intend to dress my statue in clothing that is distinctly American. I refuse to imitate Mr. Greenough's hideous example of dressing our Presidents in foreign apparel (I still bristle whenever I see his statue of George Washington in a Roman toga).

And yet, though I intend to give my statue a truly American appearance, I can't decide how to clothe Mr. Lincoln. My dilemma is thus: should I dress him in the suit he wore on the first day of his Presidency or in the theatre costume he wore on the final day of his life; should I shod his feet with boots or shoes; and should I wrap a cloak or a coat about his shoulders?

At last I thought of a solution to my dilemma. Through Senator Ross's penchant for gossip I have kept familiar with Mrs. Lincoln's travels and trials. Since her move to Chicago, she, Tad, and Robert have been living in a tiny, poorly furnished house. Supposedly Mrs. Lincoln receives no visitors and spends her hours writing letters and taking solitary walks. Her life has become dull and tragic.

Remembering Mrs. Lincoln's past kindnesses to me, I wrote her a letter to invite her suggestions and asked for the loan of one of her husband's suits so that my measurements would be accurate. I hoped my request would give some meaning to her difficult life, and I reasoned that she would know better than anyone how best to attire her husband.

She wrote back immediately. Expecting good news, I read eagerly but instead was sorely wounded by her words. Mrs. Lincoln wrote that my name to her was the name of a stranger, and she refused me the loan of any clothing.

Regina, I am distraught that Mrs. Lincoln has forgotten my sessions with her husband and my own conversations with her! Senator Ross has a theory, however—reportedly Mrs. Lincoln is terribly distressed, not only by the death of her dear husband, but from her reduced financial state. Adding to her worries are scandalous accusations from a man named Mr. Herndon, who accuses her of aiding her husband's assassins. Mr. Herndon is a known drunkard, but people are listening to him and avoiding Mrs. Lincoln.

Perhaps Mrs. Lincoln's mind is so troubled by her worries that she has forgotten me, but I am stubborn—I intend to write her often. Perhaps a word or phrase might spark her memory of my friendship with her husband, and she'll consent to the loan of a suit.

P.S.—Senator Ross has one other theory to explain why Mrs. Lincoln refuses to recognize me—one of her oldest acquaintances is none other than Mrs. Jane Swisshelm! Perhaps she is influencing Mrs. Lincoln to label me Stranger.

Thursday, November 1

Finally I have earned enough money to clean and furnish my studio. The tiled floor is spotless now, for I scrubbed until my hands grew red and raw. White paint covers the walls, upon which are hung pictures of statues. One wall is Roman, one is Greek, and one displays American statuary. The fourth wall holds my sketches of Mr. Lincoln's statue as I envision it.

In one corner, opposite the window, I have placed a harp

on a round rug of muted blues. The harp, which is carved from rosewood and decorated with inlaid ivory, was a gift from an admirer. On either side of the harp are tall racks of burnished bronze, and on the shelves are enameled pots of miniature palms. In the other corner is a narrow stove with a gay fire showing through the grate. Nearby, on a lace-covered table, I have placed the blue willow teapot you once gave me and a collection of china cups and saucers for visitors. The four chairs circling the table are softened by chintz pillows. The two remaining corners on either side of the window are lined with benches for the comfort of my guests, while above the solitary window are three bamboo cages filled with yellow canaries. The long table that came with my studio has been repainted black, and on it sit my tools and the spun-brass bowls used for mixing plaster. Beneath the table, behind a curtain of blue chintz, are bags of dry plaster.

My hours in the studio are enjoyable ones, for the room is washed with sunlight and the air is sweetened by the songs of my birds—if ever I grow weary I shall sit at my harp and accompany them as they sing.

Tuesday, Christmas Day
Another Christmas, another season of joy! My sister Mary's wedding took place yesterday evening. The ceremony was held at Major Fuller's estate in his candle-lit ballroom, a majestic room surrounded by walls of mirrors topped by wide windows. Through the glass of the undraped windows could be seen stars scattered across the winter sky.

Mary wore a simply cut, elegant gown of white satin with tiny rosebuds gathered at her waist, and her veil was of fine Irish lace caught beneath a crown of yellow roses. Mary has always been beautiful, but when she walked down the aisle her beauty looked unearthly, for her blue eyes reflected the candlelight and her golden hair glimmered like an angel's halo.

Major Fuller—I mean Perry—was clearly overcome with love when my sister joined him before their guests. He stood tall and proud, distinguished by his major's uniform with its shining sabre buckled at his side. His face, though ordinary, has one extraordinary feature: his smile. Truly he is one of the most joyous men I have ever met, and for that reason I rejoiced in my heart when he and my sister spoke their vows.

There were only a few guests, for my sister preferred an intimate ceremony. Of course Major Fuller's four little girls were there. They are darlings with their wide eyes and their tar-black curls and the sweet way they have toward my sister. All four of them—Clare, Margaret, Patricia, and little Kathleen—were frocked in lace dresses of buttercup yellow and carried porcelain baskets of winter roses.

The gown I wore, as Mary's Maiden-of-Honor, was the same color as yellow roses when first they bloom on the bush. My hair, much too long and curly to pin up, I wore tied back with a ribbon twisted with Christmas ivy. Ma looked lovely with her red hair under a veiled hat, and her gown of green velvet revealed her Scottish heritage.

Sadly, Bob could not attend the wedding because heavy snows blocked the trains coming from the Midwest. Senator Ross also missed the wedding, for he is home in Kansas for the holiday (his wife refuses to move to Washington until he can find a decent house in a respectable neighborhood).

The wedding supper was magnificent. Perry has a marvelous chef who prepared delicate dishes such as pheasant under glass and exotic vegetables curled into flowerets. The wedding cake was five tiers high and topped with sugar-cream whipped into confectionery ribbons.

My sister and her husband are away on their wedding trip. They are spending a few months in a secluded inn on St. Simon's Island off the coast of Georgia. During their long absence, Perry's daughters will be cared for by his parents.

Regina, I was amused by your lament about attending too many holiday parties. How I wish I shared your complaint—my work on the statue is never-ending, and when darkness falls I am so tired from standing all day, pushing and pressing and cutting the plaster into just the right shape, that I fall into my bed. Sometimes I even feel too weary to eat, but Ma threatens to spoon-feed me if I don't.

I did attend one Christmas Ball this season. My escort was a fascinating gentleman, but he has since returned to his University. Except for occasional suppers or concerts, I have been too weary to allow gentlemen to call often—no matter how charming they might be. And besides, dear friend, at times I still think of Boudy.

I wish you and your dear husband the very best of this season's blessings.

P.S.—In truth, I don't mind the long hours at my studio, for I am realizing my Life's Dream.

1867

1 8 6 7

Monday, *January 21*

My dear friend Regina,

My family received a cheerful note from my brother. He left Arkansas to explore Indian Territory and has since accepted work there as a government surveyor. Bob is boarding in a house that belongs to the Chickasaw tribe.

Regina, in your last letter you asked two questions. In answer to your first one—yes, dear friend, that horrible Mrs. Swisshelm continues her attack on my character. She has now declared me one of Washington's "notorious" women. She seems increasingly determined to convince her readers that I am a wicked woman who deserves contempt.

Unfortunately, Mrs. Swisshelm's colorful newspaper stories have turned my studio into a sideshow attraction! At times so many visitors—residents and tourists—crowd my studio that I cannot proceed with my work.

Many of my visitors are gentlemen who speak to me of matrimony, which amuses me, for I don't even know their names. Not an hour goes by without a proposal or two. I decline all of them respectfully—and to hide my embarrassment I do so without interrupting my work. The more persistent of the gentlemen push bouquets under my nose or recite poems meant to win my hand, but they only annoy me, for I risk making mistakes when I am distracted. Believe me when I say that mistakes in dried plaster are almost impossible to correct.

What on earth possesses those gentlemen to court me, Regina? Surely I don't present a pretty picture. Instead of a crinoline gown with my hair pinned and perfumed, I wear a rough dress and apron, dusted with powder and splattered with wet plaster, and my shoes are my old school-girl shoes with the rubber toes (the plaster ruins clothing and leather, so I prefer this costume). And yet the parade of suitors never ends. Perhaps they are not seeing me as I am, but rather as the "notorious" lady of Mrs. Swisshelm's distorted imagination.

Mostly I am amused, though, and sometimes even flattered by the tenacity of my suitors, but I am always annoyed by the proposals I receive through the mail. On average a dozen such letters arrive each day. So, although I arrive home at night weary with hands aching from sculpting, I must sit down at once and write letters of rejection. Last week I received a proposal from Mr. Brigham Young, the leader of the Mormons, to join his collection of wives. That rejection took an hour to compose, for I am ignorant of his beliefs and labored over my words so as not to offend him.

And in answer to your second question—yes, dear friend, I have read the articles written by the journalists who kindly defend me against Mrs. Swisshelm. I was especially amused by the writer who described me as a "mature Botticelli cherub." Perhaps that reporter noticed the harp sitting in a corner of my studio and my dove, Poet, who always perches on my shoulder as I sculpt.

I do wish Mrs. Swisshelm would grow weary of attacking me with her Poison Pen. Perhaps if she ceased her criticisms I would cease to be such a curiosity to those who wish to look upon and wed a "notorious" woman.

P.S.—I meant to tell you in my last letter and I nearly forgot again: I have written thrice more to Mrs. Lincoln for the loan of her husband's clothing, and her reply each time has been a firm no. I shall write her again tonight.

Friday, March 1
My work in the studio is never labor but an ecstatic delight to

my soul. Although the hours pass quickly and happily, my progress is slow, for I must pause quite often to prepare fresh bowls of plaster.

Wet plaster is simple to prepare. First, I fill a spun-brass bowl with water, sprinkle in dry plaster, and then place my hand at the bottom of the bowl so as to move my fingers back and forth to blend the mixture. Each time I take care to pop every air bubble and crush each lump, for they could cause weak spots in the plaster when it hardens. Usually I add pieces of burlap to thicken the mixture, and after about ten minutes the stuff changes enough so that I can begin modeling.

It is then, Regina, that the plaster is most similar to clay, but instead of using my fingers to mold, I use a spatula. For thirty wonderful minutes I sculpt, but when the plaster begins to harden I use a knife, a scraper, or a rasp to smooth and grate off layers of the plaster or to add texture to the piece. When another half hour passes, the plaster hardens completely as the water in the mixture disappears, making further changes almost impossible. Thus, Regina, I must carefully plan what to cut or scrape before the moment of hardening.

Wouldn't it be wonderful if I could invent a machine to mix the plaster for me! Ma says she wishes she could invent a machine to wash the plaster stains from my dresses!

Friday, April 5

I have happy news to share. My family received another long letter from Bob telling us that he is pleased with his decision to go West. He wrote pages of detailed descriptions about the unmapped regions he has surveyed for the government, and then for several more pages he described a Chickasaw maiden named Anna Guy—her beauty, her gentleness, her voice, her laughter, her intelligence, and her honored work as a teacher. As we continued to read Bob's letter we realized that he was in love with her. And then, at the very close of his letter, he startled us with the announcement that he and Anna had married!

My parents, Mary, and I are overjoyed, as you can well imagine.

My brother and his wife are staying with Anna's family until Bob can build them a home on her father's land. He and Anna's brothers have already begun digging the foundation.

Regina, am I destined to remain the only unmarried one of us all? Of late, the only gentlemen I meet are those enticed to my studio by Mrs. Swisshelm's articles. Surely none of them are in love with me—they are in love with a "notorious" sculptress named Vinnie Ream.

P.S.—Your description of the fountains of Salzburg has inspired me—I shall paint a picture of those fountains and send it to Bob and Anna as a wedding gift.

Tuesday, April 16
This morning I had just unlocked the door of my studio when a gentleman named Mr. Alphonso Dunn called on me. He had worked at the White House during Mr. Lincoln's administration and works there now under President Johnson. In Mr. Dunn's hands was a huge box containing some of Mr. Lincoln's clothes—a fine suit, a pair of his giant shoes, and a cloak that he once wore to the theatre.

My visitor explained that after Mr. Lincoln's death his widow bequeathed many of his personal possessions to those who had demonstrated their love for her husband. Mrs. Lincoln gave this particular collection of clothes to Mr. Dunn. Recently she wrote him of my repeated requests to borrow her husband's clothes, and in turn he came to see me.

I thanked Mr. Dunn for his generous loan and assured him that Mr. Lincoln's clothes would be guarded with my life.

Finally, Regina, I know how to drape the statue! Mr. Lincoln will be dressed as a true American.

P.S.—As you know, my dove, Poet, sits on my right shoulder while I sculpt. Mr. Dunn must be superstitious, for upon seeing Poet alight on my shoulder he declared the sight an omen that my statue will succeed. I didn't want to disappoint him by explaining that Poet is trained, not wild.

Saturday, May 11

This afternoon I received another letter proposing marriage, but this time I nearly accepted the proposal—the writer of the letter was Boudy. Boudy wrote that he loves me, that he has always loved me, that he will always love me, and as I read his words of love my heart felt like a rose blooming beneath a warm sun— but then I read the last line of his letter and my heart withered and dried to dust. Boudy's final words were, "Abandon your foolish notion of sculpting. Why waste your days laboring over the form of a man who resembled a gorilla in face and act."

Oh, Regina, how could Boudy profess to love me and yet mock my reverence for our Martyr President? And how could he claim he loves me and yet dismiss my desire to sculpt as a "foolish notion"?

How different Boudy is from his cousin! John's letters offer tender words of encouragement, for he respects my desire to honor Mr. Lincoln's memory through my sculpture. John understands and appreciates my dream of being a sculptress.

I have written to Boudy and refused his offer of matrimony. My refusal will pierce his proud heart, and I doubt he will ever write me again. Perhaps that would be better, for if he persists in courting me, I might, in a weak moment, abandon sculpting to revive my withered heart.

Saturday, July 20

This afternoon I was mixing a bowl of plaster when a gentleman appeared at my studio door. Leaning on a crutch, he frowned at me so harshly that I felt affrighted. Indeed he had a most unpleasant look, for his stern face lacked color and bore the marks of recent illness. His brows were so thick that they almost obscured his sickly eyes, and his mouth was deeply creased at the corners as though he rarely smiled. He wore on his head an unbecoming brown wig, and on the wig sat an old-fashioned hat. The poor man was burdened by a club foot, which explained his crutch, and his veined hands shook slightly. I stared at him with some trepidation until I realized who he was—Pennsylvania Representative Thaddeus Stevens, the most powerful man in Congress. Wiping the plaster from my hands I welcomed him into my studio.

Congressman Stevens' voice should have put fear in my heart, but I had heard that he suffers with never-ending pain, so I ignored his gruff tone. He told me that he had been approached by a group of ladies who had accused me of serious crimes. I asked him to name those crimes.

He looked about my studio before settling his pale eyes on my face. "Your first crime," he said, "is that your studio is a pleasant place filled with birds and flowers."

I thought I had misheard him, but I listened without comment.

"Your second crime," he said, "is that you wear your hair long and unbound."

I gasped at that as he went on, "But your chief crime is that your face is attracting gentlemen to your studio."

I started to defend myself, but before I spoke he laughed merrily, his laughter echoing around the room. He laughed so heartily that he broke into a fit of coughing and, weakened, grasped at my arm. Alarmed that he was ill, I led him over to a chair and poured him tea.

The honeyed tea calmed his cough, and after a while he smiled at me and revealed the purpose of his visit. It seems, Regina, that my accusers, a group of women who have joined Mrs. Swisshelm's war against me, demanded that Mr. Stevens use his position in Congress to close my studio and destroy my sculpture.

Mr. Stevens and I laughed at the charges against me and then spoke of more serious subjects. He learned of my devotion to Mr. Lincoln, and I learned of his passionate hatred for President Johnson. As the pleasant hour passed we recognized in each other our devotion to our Nation, but whereas Mr. Stevens proclaims his devotion through his work in Congress, I proclaim mine through my sculpting.

Later, before the good man took his leave, he held my hands in his and said, "Miss Ream, jealousy causes many to speak cruelly about those they envy. Through no fault of your own, but Nature's, you have earned the wrath of creatures corrupted by jealousy."

Though flattered by his words, I was also terrified by their meaning. Oh, Regina, will those spiteful women succeed in destroying my statue?

When I was alone, I bolted the door of my studio and sat at my harp. The music soothed my soul, as did the singing of my sweet canaries, but it was nearing midnight before I put on my cape and walked slowly home. Regina, no matter how hard I try, I cannot rid myself of the fear that my statue will never be completed.

Wednesday, August 7

Boudy has written a final letter asking me to abandon my sculpture and wed him at summer's end. I wrote back at once, before my heart weakened. Oh, Regina, perhaps I could live without sculpting, but I could never live with a husband whose heart has turned to stone. And yet I love him. I always will.

Write to me, dear friend, and tell if I chose wisely.

Tuesday, September 24

Thank you, dear Regina, for your birthday gift. When next I return to my studio I shall play the songs on my harp—truly there is a haunting quality about the Celtic music of Ireland.

This evening my parents and I dined at Mary's home. We ate a delicious supper of roasted hen and potatoes baked in butter and a dessert of lemon cake, and then I received the most wonderful gift imaginable. My darling sister revealed a secret— she is with child!

Oh, Regina, you cannot imagine my family's joy. Ma is already choosing yarns to knit tiny boots and caps, and Pa is designing a cradle that he will build himself. And I haven't stopped smiling since my sister asked me to be the child's godmother.

My sister and her husband have known about Mary's condition for two weeks, but Mary wanted to save her happy news for my birthday celebration. She said that she had trouble keeping her marvelous secret from her daughters, but now that they know, they are bursting with excitement.

Regina, I know that you and Michael are preparing for your

return to New York City, and so this will be my final letter to you until your arrival home from Europe. Have a wonderful voyage, dear friend. When you return we must visit, for I am anxious to meet your husband.

P.S.—Just imagine, Regina, by summer I will be an aunt! I hope that if the child is a girl she inherits my sister's beauty and grace.

Friday, October 11

My work is proceeding slowly, very slowly, because I haven't the heart to turn away the hordes of visitors that gather in my studio. After all, it is their taxes that will pay my commission, if my work is approved.

If—if my work is approved. It is highly possible that my statue will be ridiculed and scorned and then these many months of hard work will have been for nothing. Each day when I arrive at my studio I look at what I have done and compare that to what I must do, and the task seems impossible. Perhaps Mrs. Swisshelm is right. Why should I, a novice sculptress, believe that I can accomplish the Herculean task of turning dry plaster into living man?

Oh, Regina, I cannot fail. I dare not fail. The citizens of this country are depending on me to create a statue equal to their memory of our dear Mr. Lincoln.

There is another reason that I dare not fail. Pa is that reason. Even though he works only half days, he is worn with fatigue. If my vision of the statue is fulfilled—if the government approves of my work—if the public accepts my memorial—then and only then will I be awarded the money that would allow Pa the financial freedom to retire. If only that could happen! I dream of such a day when my parents and I can sail off to Europe, for I know Pa's health would be restored on the sun-drenched beaches of Italy.

Saturday, November 30

I just opened your letter and read of your arrival in New York City. I am relieved that your crossing over the ocean was uneventful, but I am distressed by the news of your illness. It is unnatural that your back should ache so painfully, unnatural too that you sicken at the very smell of food. I urge you to seek out the finest doctor in New York City, and then, dear friend, please write me at your first opportunity.

Until then, know that you are in my daily thoughts and prayers.

Wednesday, Christmas Day

I am delighted to learn the cause of your illness! Oh, Regina, I can hardly believe that you are carrying your first child! What marvelous news! There is no better way to celebrate Christmas than to know that within you is the most precious gift of all—a new life.

How wise of you to listen to your doctor. Surround yourself with books and embroidery and your confinement won't seem overlong. Ma believes your bouts of nausea and backaches may disappear, but she agrees with your doctor's orders to stay quiet until you regain your strength. Ma suggests, too, that you drink green tea. She once heard that women in the Orient drink pots of green tea and the moment they give birth they return to their work in rice fields. Perhaps a cup or two of green tea would restore your lost strength.

As for my sister's condition—no, Regina, Mary has not suffered the pains you described, nor has she complained of weakness or headaches. My sister has had some strange desires, though, for foods that are rather ghastly. Yesterday she ate chocolate covered with garlic paste.

This festive season is passing quickly. I have taken a brief holiday from sculpting to attend Washington's Christmas Ball and other dances and holiday concerts. I have a different escort for each occasion, for I have decided that I cannot allow myself to become betrothed until my statue is completed.

This year approaches its end without another letter from Boudy, but in truth I knew he'd never write again. Rarely do I think of him now, except in unguarded moments when I recall the darkness of his eyes or the richness of his voice. At those moments I force myself to remember, too, the anger that clouds his eyes and the hatred that has changed his voice.

Regina, in one week a new year will be ushered in. Ever since I was a small girl I have wished on the first star I see in the New Year's sky. This year my wishes will be many.

I will wish that the New Year brings months of quietude so that my statue can be completed.

I will wish that the New Year allows me the chance to finally visit you—how I long to meet your sweet husband.

I will wish that the New Year brings my brother and his wife here to Washington for a long, long visit.

I will wish that you and Mary are blessed with healthy, beautiful babies.

And I will whisper to the stars one final wish—I will wish that Boudy quenches the fiery anger that has changed him from the man I once longed to marry, to a man I could never wed.

Remember me on New Year's Eve, Regina, and if the sky is starry that night, think of me standing beneath those stars, wishing with all my heart.

1868

1 8 6 8

Tuesday, January 21

My dear friend Regina,

This morning I received a telegram from Boudy. His message was brief. He wrote, "John died this afternoon. Will write soon."

I read Boudy's message over and over and over again, refusing to believe what I was reading. I knew it had to be true, though, for Boudy loved his cousin as much as I and would never have written such a painful message in jest.

I heard my parents' voices in the kitchen, but I needed to be alone, and so I fled through the front door to the streets of Washington. I'm not sure how long I walked, Regina, or where I walked, but somehow I ended up at my studio and I bolted the door to keep out visitors.

For a long while I sat near the harp, not playing a note, just staring at the strings shining like gold in the morning sun. As I watched, the sun's light moved through the strings and across the floor and touched my unfinished statue.

Did I ever tell you, Regina, that John's recent letters never failed to make mention of my work on the statue? He had never seen my sculpture, of course, and yet his letters sounded as though he had personally visited my studio and was familiar with my daily progress. Oh, Regina, how I will miss John's notes of encouragement. How I will miss him.

All day today I worked on my statue with a fury I have never known. I mixed bowl after bowl of plaster and pressed and cut and scraped away the stuff until my hands ached and my back hurt. And still I worked until the sun faded in the sky and night darkened my window. I worked on and on, for I felt as though John stood there beside me, watching me with his gentle eyes, smiling at his dove sitting on my shoulder, nodding his head with approval of my effort. I worked and I worked and I worked until, at some point, I realized someone was pounding at my door.

It was my father, worried about my long absence from home. In simple words I told him about John. Pa didn't say a word. There was no need for words as he cradled me in his arms and I wept.

Our walk home was slow, despite the lateness of the hour and the cold that crept through our coats. We spoke about John, remembering his kindness, reciting bits of his poetry, laughing and crying and sometimes just walking in silence.

The hour has grown very late. Pa is sitting with Ma by the hearth and I am writing this letter to you, dear friend, in my attic room—my parents believe I'm asleep, but sleep is impossible.

Do you remember the poem John wrote for me when I was a mere child of thirteen? Just last week I received a letter from him—in that letter his words of love echoed the same words of love he wrote to me seven long years ago. How is it possible, Regina, that as a small girl I managed to capture the heart of that gentle, gentle man, and how is it possible that I was able to hold his gentle heart captive these many, many years?

Tuesday, February 11

Today my family received two letters, one from Boudy and the other from my brother. Boudy wrote about John's death. Oh, Regina, John died from the dreaded tuberculosis. We knew that John had once suffered from that disease, but we thought him cured. Sadly, his illness returned with a vengeance. Last October John spat up blood and knew at once that he was dying. He confided in his cousin, Boudy, but he kept his terrible secret of approaching death from me. Boudy explained that

John worried that my knowing of his illness might distract me from my sculpting. Oh, Regina, John loved me so much. Much more than I deserved.

My brother's letter brought happy news. Bob and his wife, Anna, have a son and daughter. Yes, Regina, twins! Anna wanted to keep her condition from us, for she suffered with months of illness and wanted to spare us from worry. All her fears were for naught, for she bore fat, healthy babies blessed with Anna's dark hair and our mother's wide eyes. They have named their son Boudinot, after Boudy, and their daughter Vinnie, which honors me deeply. Needless to say, the arrival of grand-children in my family has caused much happiness.

Is it not strange, dear friend, how nature balances itself —the death of a gentle man balanced by the birth of gentle children—the heartache of Death balanced by the joy of Birth.

Thursday, March 5

My custom is to leave for my studio before dawn. In the silence of the darkened streets I think about the statue and plan my next step. When I arrive at the Capitol, the guard unlocks the front doors and I hurry through the empty hallways to my stu-dio. Except for the girls mopping the floors, the building remains quiet for hours. I welcome these peaceful hours, for I can complete much work on the statue before the chambers fill up with the noise of cursing, shouting, and stomping feet—the Impeachment Trial of President Johnson has begun!

Do you remember my recent letter about Representative Thaddeus Stevens? He and his fellow Republicans, who call themselves Radicals, are determined to destroy Andrew Johnson.

It seems, dear friend, that President Johnson has followed Abraham Lincoln's notion of forgiving the states that rebelled, but the Radicals wish to punish the South. To do so, they plan to force President Johnson from office and so they have accused him of a crime: they have declared his removal of the Secretary of War, Mr. Edwin Stanton, an illegal act. Mr. Stanton refuses to give up his position—for weeks he has barricaded himself in his office.

Three years ago, when my brother first came home from the War, I wrote that his arrival was a sign that Everlasting Peace had come to our Nation. How foolish and naive I was to have believed that! I dread the days to come.

Thursday, March 19

Our Nation's troubles have entrapped me like a moth drawn into a spider's sticky web. This morning, in the hour before dawn, I left as usual for my studio. I had not walked far when I heard footsteps behind me. Turning, I saw no one, for the darkness was thickened by grey fog, and yet when I paused the footsteps paused too. I quickened my step, and the footsteps behind me quickened as well. Instinct warned me of danger, but there was no one around who could help. Windows were draped and dark. There were no policemen, no street vendors— no one at all.

My heart thrashed against my chest as I ran wildly through the fog-drenched streets. Even as I ran I could hear boots pounding behind me. I ran faster and faster until the marble steps of the Capitol lay under my shoes. Up the steps I flew, and only when I had reached the top and could see the guard unlocking the door to let me in did I feel safe. Gasping for breath, I spun around to see the face of the demon who had chased me.

In the dim light cast from a lamp, I clearly saw the man's

face. He stood so close to me that I could hear his labored breathing, I could smell his sour breath. I stared at him for only the briefest of moments, but never will I forget his face. He had long, yellow teeth that hung over his bottom lip and a nose as thin as a nail. His eyes were bloodshot and his hair sprouted out like a bush of grey wire. He wore a baggy overcoat that stunk of wet horsehair and a felt hat that fell over one eye. All that I saw in the brief moment before I screamed.

Even as the guard rushed towards me, that villain darted back down the steps, but in his haste he dropped a black book. When he had disappeared down the street I picked up the book, and later, behind the locked door of my studio, I read every page. Horrified, I learned that he had been following me for days. In a shaky hand he had recorded my every move—my hours at the studio, my walks with Ma, my visits with Pa to Mary's home, my evenings at the theatre with escorts. His interest puzzled me, but his final entry frightened me, for he had written: "V. Ream has much to lose—she'll help us win over E. Ross."

You can imagine how I dashed upstairs to Senator Ross's office to await his arrival. Even before he greeted me, I showed him the book, and he startled me with the news that he too is being followed.

It seems, Regina, that the Radical Republicans have turned against him, even though he himself is one of their group. They are infuriated by his belief that President Johnson is entitled to a fair trial. Since the Radicals need a two-thirds majority, thirty-six votes, in order to remove President Johnson from office—and only thirty-five senators have promised to vote guilty—they are depending on Senator Ross's vote.

The Radicals' spies are devious. Having discovered that Senator Ross's brother was in need of money, they offered him

$20,000 to influence his brother's vote. He refused the bribe, so now those spies are targeting me with their evil. What will I lose if I don't help them? My life? Oh, Regina, I feel like that entangled moth awaiting the venomous spider.

Saturday, March 28

I wasn't surprised to learn that you've read critical articles about Senator Ross in your New York newspapers. Ours also are denouncing him as a traitor to his fellow Radicals.

Ma dreads the day the Impeachment Trial closes, for she fears for the senator's safety. Every day cruel, hateful messages are left on our front step—messages threatening beatings or even murder if the senator doesn't vote for Johnson's removal. One letter enclosed a crude drawing of Senator Ross hanged by his neck on a gallows, and beneath the gruesome picture was printed, "This happens to traitors who vote the wrong way." Last night a letter, smeared with fresh blood, was tied to a brick and thrown through our parlor window.

In a corner of our dining room sits a huge bag bulging with telegrams from the citizens of Kansas, Senator Ross's home state. They are demanding that he either support the Radicals or risk suffering as an Enemy of Kansas.

Every waking day is fraught with difficulties for Senator Ross. He ignores the spies following him, for there is nothing in his past or present life that he wishes to hide. He ignores, too, the rude comments made by his fellow senators and their angry exclusion of him in Society. But there is one matter he finds difficult to ignore—the belligerence of ordinary citizens. Senator Ross cannot walk anywhere in this city without someone spitting in his face, or flinging mud and stones at him, or threatening him with fists or weapons. And yet, throughout all this abuse, Senator Ross refuses to reveal to anyone how he intends to vote (even Pa doesn't know). He is determined to keep his silence until after he has heard all of the evidence against President Johnson.

I have also learned to ignore that brute who spies on me. I have decided, however, that if he ever speaks to me I will forget for the moment that I am a lady.

Wednesday, April 1

It is hours past midnight, but sleep refuses to come—please ignore my untidy penmanship, for the words are tumbling excitedly from my pen.

After supper tonight, Pa and I went to my studio to repair a bench that had split. Around eight o'clock we heard soft knocking. It was Senator Ross and six other Republicans, who entered quickly and then bolted the door (one of them was Senator Trumbull, that kind gentleman who told Mr. Lincoln of my desire to sculpt him). The senators asked permission to use my studio for a secret meeting, and I agreed at once. While Pa hammered and I prepared tea for the gentlemen, the senators sat in a circle and discussed the impeachment in low voices.

After some time they invited Pa and me to join their discussion. We sat until midnight debating the guilt or innocence of our President. I made my opinion known, that the President is good and great in his understanding that if we welcome our Southern states back into our Union without bitterness, our Nation's wounds will heal more quickly.

On leaving tonight the senators asked for liberty to use my studio whenever they must meet in secret, and again I agreed at once.

Monday, April 20

Early this morning that dreadful man who has been spying on me walked boldly into my studio. Behind him strode another man, a person of obvious wealth, for he wore a fine suit and carried a silver-capped walking stick. Despite the elegance of his suit I would not label him a gentleman because of the rude way he spoke to me. He didn't introduce himself by name, but I recognized him as Representative Benjamin Butler, one of the managers of the Radicals' movement. In Washington he is called the Beast, not only because his appearance is beast-like (he resembles a walrus with his shiny bald head and his slitted eyes and droopy mustache), but because of his cruel and merciless nature.

The spy closed and bolted the door of my studio, and then he stood before it as he pulled a wad of chewing tobacco from his pocket.

The Beast came over to me. There was no expression on his face, but his eyes flashed with anger when he told me that the Radicals knew of the secret meetings in my studio. His voice sharpened like a butcher's knife when he told me that I must use feminine wiles to influence Senator Ross's vote. If I refused, Mr. Butler threatened to break my statue and lock me out of my studio.

My heart thudded. I clasped my hands together to hide their trembling, and lifting my chin I looked that uncouth man directly in his eyes. Struggling to keep my voice even, I told him that my respect for Senator Ross prohibited me from doing as he asked.

My little speech of defiance did not impress Mr. Butler. He reminded me that unless I had a statue to show the govern-ment, I would not be paid for my work. His narrow eyes darted towards the man in the horsehair coat, who came over to me and spat tobacco juice at the hem of my dress. Then, picking up a bowl of wet plaster, the man threw it against the wall before he went over and unlocked the door. As Mr. Butler turned to go, he shook his cane at me and uttered one final warning that I must heed his words.

Dear friend, I am overwrought with fear. If Mr. Butler has the means to destroy my statue, my dream of honoring Mr. Lincoln will never be realized. And my dream of providing Pa and Ma with financial freedom would also fade away. And yet I cannot—I will not—allow the Radicals to abuse my friendship with Senator Ross. He is an honorable man and must be allowed to cast his vote as he wishes.

I have decided not to tell my family or Senator Ross about Mr. Butler's threats. If Ma knew, she'd insist that I close my studio at once. Regina, I need your advice—should I report Mr. Butler's brutish threats to the police, or should I stay quiet and hope that beastly man forgets that I exist? Please, Regina, write me without delay.

Saturday, May 2

Late last night I arrived home to find my parents and Senator Ross gathered in the darkened parlor. In lowered voices they told me that the carriage of General Sickles was parked near our front door. Senator Ross suspected that General Sickles had been sent by the Radicals to keep him from attending a secret meeting across town—an important meeting to discuss the final evidence in President Johnson's trial. The problem was how to sneak Senator Ross past the general without being seen (the back door was useless, as the general's aide stood guard there).

Ma came up with the solution. Her proposal surprised us all, for she is a genteel lady not given to intrigue. Ma had heard rumors that the general, despite his advanced years, was easily distracted by a woman's face. Ma's idea was that I should go out into the street and charm him away from our door.

I fastened my cape around my shoulders and hurried out into the night. Smiling up at the general, I asked him for a word in private, and he descended to the street and asked me to speak. I hesitated, glancing over at his driver as if I didn't want my words overheard. General Sickles misunderstood my flirtatious smile, as I had hoped, and ordered his driver to walk the horse down the street. The moment his carriage passed by, I took the general's arm and, prattling about nonsensical things, led him casually away from my house. Out of the corner of my eye I saw my front door inching open and Senator Ross stepping quietly to the pavement and vanishing into the shadows of night.

I waited a few minutes more, feigning interest in General Sickles' comments, but when I judged my chore completed, I released his arm and bade him good night. General Sickles seemed startled by my sudden leave-taking, but then he noticed Pa and Ma standing in the open door and understood at once that we had made a fool of him. Without another word, he stalked off towards his waiting carriage.

That was last night. This morning I found my studio unlocked. Alarmed, I pushed the door wide and was sickened by what I saw.

Regina, dozens of bags of dry plaster had been knifed open; the powdery stuff covered the entire floor. The harp lay on its side, and the palms had been dumped out of their pots. The cages of my canaries and my dove, Poet, had been pulled down and smashed. (My birds, thank heavens, were unharmed; they flew about in wild confusion.) And yet there was worse, much worse—the statue of our dear Mr. Lincoln was stained with splotches of tobacco juice.

My studio is again in order. I know, of course, the creatures responsible for the heinous act—that brutish man in the horsehair coat and his master, Mr. Butler. It is obvious they were displeased with me for making a fool of their agent, General Sickles.

Saturday, May 16

Last night General Sickles again knocked at our door, but this time Senator Ross was hidden miles away in the home of an old friend. General Sickles, refusing to believe that the senator was away for the night, sat stubbornly on Ma's red sofa until the break of dawn.

This morning the Radicals' spies traced Senator Ross to his breakfast table and escorted him to the Capitol. Pa and I were waiting for him there, for we wanted to support him with our presence. Today was the day that the senators finally cast their votes to decide the innocence or guilt of President Johnson.

Before the voting began, Pa and I met Senator Ross in the lobby to wish him well. As we spoke, Representative Thaddeus Stevens came over to us. He leaned heavily on his crutch and I pitied him his weakness, but when he spoke to Senator Ross he sounded powerfully strong. He said, "Let me look on the face of a man who might cast his vote in support of that criminal named Johnson."

I shuddered at the hatred evident in Mr. Stevens' voice, and then, at that very moment, one of Senator Ross's colleagues from Kansas strode towards him, grabbed him by his lapels, and threatened to bury him in his political grave if he didn't vote with the Radicals. Senator Ross removed the man's hands from his coat and told him in a flat, even tone that he intended to vote as would best serve our Nation.

Expecting the two men to turn to their fists, Pa hurried me away to our seats in the gallery overlooking the Senate's Chamber. The gallery was thronged with gentlemen and ladies, all of whom had to pay dearly for their tickets (my brother-in-law generously provided tickets for Pa and me). We found our seats in the first row and leaned over the railing.

Below us, on the floor of the Chamber, all fifty-four senators from the twenty-seven states were present and seated. (The Southern states have of course not yet been recognized again since their secession, and therefore were not given seats.) A gentleman beside me pointed out the very ill Senator from Iowa who had to be carried in and propped in his chair. We watched as other chairs were carried in for members of the President's Cabinet and Representatives of the House.

Before the Chief Justice began the roll call of senators to record their votes, he warned us, the audience in the gallery, to keep absolute silence. Indeed, Regina, silence reigned supreme in the gallery as one by one the senators called out their votes, guilty or not guilty. By the time the Chief Justice called out the state of Kansas, the air in the chamber felt as electric as the air before a lightning storm. In the unearthly quiet, I couldn't hear a petticoat rustle or a gentleman cough or a chair creak. Indeed, as I glanced around the gallery it seemed that everyone had frozen, their angry faces turned down towards Senator Ross. And he, dear friend, he sat white-faced like a statue of marble under the glare of hundreds of hostile eyes.

Senator Ross's name was called. He hesitated, noisily clearing his throat. Every politician seated on the Senate floor turned towards him. The silence was the silence of a tomb, and yet when he spoke I couldn't hear his vote. I doubt anyone in the gallery had heard, but no one dared protest. Below us, enraged senators throughout the chamber demanded that Senator Ross repeat his vote. And so he did, thrusting his voice into the far corners of the room. "Not guilty," he shouted.

The deathly silence deepened—if such a thing were possible—as the roll call continued and other senators cast their votes. But it was over. Without the senator's vote, the Radicals failed to gather the necessary thirty-six votes to find the President guilty. Senator Ross's act of bravery, his one vote, has saved the presidency of Andrew Johnson.

At supper we were hesitant to speak about the trial, for the senator is sorely troubled—not about his decision, but about the bleakness of his future. Later, as we settled by the hearth with our coffee, he sighed and said, "When I was waiting to cast my vote I literally looked down into my open grave." Oh, Regina, when Senator Ross uttered the two words "not guilty," he knew that he cast away friendships and position and fortune.

Pa asked his friend what had made him decide to cast that vote, and he told us this—he realized that if President Johnson had been removed from office simply for disagreeing with Congress, then every President in our Nation's future would risk such a fate for any minor disagreement with Congress. In essence, the balance of power would cease to exist.

Senator Ross still sits by the hearth writing a letter to his wife. He intends to resign at the end of his term, for he knows that from the political grave into which he has fallen there is no resurrection.

Monday, May 18
I received your letter of advice just in time. This morning I

arrived at my studio to find the door chained and padlocked. A large sign had been posted which read, "Studio A—Closed Permanently." Heeding your advice, Regina, I hastened at once to the office of Representative Thaddeus Stevens.

Although the hour was early he sat hunched over his desk, his worn face made masklike by the pallid color of ill health. When he noticed me at his door a frown creased his eyes as he said, "Your good friend Senator Ross deserted his fellow Republicans yesterday."

In a low voice I reminded him that I had no part in Senator Ross's vote.

Mr. Stevens scowled at my reply, but I overlooked his bad temper and in a rush of emotion explained my purpose in seeking him out. He listened with gracious patience and then, taking up his crutch, returned with me to my studio. There he cursed under his breath, ripped down the sign, and threw it on the floor. Then, offering his arm, he walked me back upstairs and we began a round of visits to the offices of important gentlemen.

Regina, what happened next amazed me. By the time night had fallen we had a petition endorsing my work, signed by President Andrew Johnson, three of his Cabinet officials, 105 congressmen and 31 senators, General Ulysses S. Grant and General George Custer, and several sculptors, including my teacher, Mr. Clark Mills!

At the top of the petition Mr. Stevens had written, "We the undersigned have a national pride in Miss Ream ... and we support development of her unquestionable genius." His kind words flattered me immensely, as did the distinguished signatures affixed to the petition.

I am in my studio as I write this letter to you, dear friend, to thank you for your wise counsel to seek out the assistance of Mr. Stevens. How charitable of him to help me even though his arch-enemy, President Johnson, was saved by my good friend Senator Ross. I intend to repay Mr. Stevens' kind deed by sculpting his head in clay—I will capture his fierce scowl, but I will also capture the goodness that adds brightness to his sickly eyes.

Monday, June 22

I have wonderful news to share. Early this morning Mary became the mother of a beautiful, healthy girl. Oh, Regina, she is so tiny—her face is a small circle and her head is crowned with golden curls as soft as lamb's wool. As yet she hasn't opened her eyes, but she makes the most delightful faces in her sleep. She is named Lavinia, after my mother. My sister is resting comfortably with her daughter at her side, and Perry is passing out Cuban cigars to everyone he sees.

Ma cried when she first saw her granddaughter, for she swears that Lavinia is the very image of Mary as a wee baby. If little Lavinia has inherited my sister's sweetness and beauty and her father's joy and laughter, then she has been blessed a hundredfold.

I must close now, for Pa and I have promised to take Mary's daughters shopping for gifts for their new sister.

P.S.—Very soon, dear friend, you, too, will be cradling your own little one close to your heart.

Monday, July 20

Your last letter alarmed me. Regina, you must listen to your doctor! If he believes you should stay abed until your baby is born, you must heed his advice.

Forgive my harsh tone, but please do not be stubborn,

Regina. Ma has heard of pregnancies such as yours and worries that if you ignore your doctor's wishes you risk much.

Please take to your bed and enjoy your hours of solitude. Read the books you have never had time for, or embroider in peace without the daily interruptions of household affairs. Be thankful that your husband has found you maids and nurses whom you can trust. Why be mulish? Do whatever is necessary to ensure your baby's health.

And remember, dear friend, that you and your unborn child remain in my family's daily prayers.

P.S.—Ma said that you shouldn't fret about your swollen feet and fingers. Soon after you give birth you will again wear fashionable shoes, and your wedding band will fit as perfectly as on the day you were wed.

Monday, August 3

I received your brief letter explaining the blurring of your vision. Try not to worry, Regina, and try not to lose faith in your doctor. Surely clear sight will return as he promises— after your baby is born all your symptoms will disappear. Take courage that Michael is never far from your side and that your nurses are attentive to your every need.

What a terrible hardship it must be for you, dear friend, to be confined to your bed without vision enough for reading novels or embroidering. I am glad that we are able to continue our correspondence in spite of your reduced vision (how good of your husband to write your letters to me, and how good of him to read my letters aloud to you!).

I sympathize with your boredom. Enclosed is a slim book of William Shakespeare's sonnets, for I have never forgotten how much you once enjoyed his poetry. Could there be a better way to pass long hours than to listen to your sweet husband reading poems of love?

Rest well, dear friend, and remember that you are in my prayers and thoughts, for I treasure you as though you were my other sister.

Monday, August 17

Your husband wrote me about your worsened condition, about the terrible weakness that drains you of strength to sit or eat or even speak. Michael also wrote that you have convinced yourself that you and your unborn child are dying.

Oh, Regina, how wretched I feel that the distance between our homes prevents me from taking you by the hand and pleading with you to deny those thoughts of death. I am reduced to pleading with you through this letter, so listen carefully, Regina, to my every plea.

I plead with you not to dwell on Death or surely Death will conquer you.

I plead with you to think instead of your Precious Child and the joys you both will share.

I plead with you to find the strength to eat something, anything at all, to nourish yourself and the child within you.

And I plead with you not to lose hope. Regina, struggle to survive. Please, Regina, struggle!

We are separated by miles, dear friend, but know that you are near me in heart. And know that my every thought and every prayer is for you, for Michael, and for the child you carry.

Friday, September 4

I wept with sheer joy when I read your letter—twins! How lucky I am to share the wonder of twins twice in my life, my brother's twins and now yours! Dear friend, you are blessed twice over by the birth of two babies. What lovely names you have chosen. If your parents were still alive they would be proud to know their grandchildren bore their names.

I was glad to hear that your aunt and uncle were visiting at your time of confinement. Give my love to them and to your husband and kiss your precious babies for me.

I am honored that you and Michael have chosen me as godmother for both Johnny and Nellie. And thank you for postponing the Christening until I can visit New York City. I will come in the springtime the moment my statue is completed.

My parents and sister send their best wishes. Ma had already knitted you a Christening blanket and now she is hurriedly knitting another.

P.S.—Now your months of discomfort and weakness are explained. Surely carrying two babies would tax any woman's strength, especially babies as large as yours.

Thursday, September 24

This has been a birthday I shall never forget—for reasons you will soon understand. As is well known, Mr. Lincoln was exceptionally tall for a gentleman, and I, much to my chagrin, have never grown past four feet, ten inches. Thus, to sculpt Mr. Lincoln's shoulders, I had to erect a scaffold, a wooden plank braced between iron poles. Several days ago I fell off the plank and landed on my head. Unfortunately, for once I had no visitors, and before I was discovered my wound bled quite freely. How long I lay on the floor before my discovery could not be determined, for I was unconscious.

I was carried by cart to my home and remained in that

sleeplike state for nearly twenty hours, during which time my poor mother grew frantic and wired my brother to come home at once. When I awoke, a bit groggy but very much alive, Pa sent another telegram to Bob to tell him the crisis had ended, but it was too late—he had already left by train.

My distraught brother arrived in Washington expecting to attend my funeral, but instead he arrived in time for my birthday celebration. Bob brought precious gifts—his exquisite wife and their beautiful children.

Oh, Regina, you should see little Boudinot and Vinnie. They crawl everywhere and climb on everything, which amuses me from the sofa I am forced to rest upon (my head still aches from the fall off the scaffold). Often I sing to them the lullabies Ma once sang, and their smiles are like sweet applause.

As I look upon my brother's twins I am reminded of your twins—how I long to sing to them!

I must close now, for my family is waiting for me downstairs. The sounds of their laughter and voices are floating up the steps like chords of the sweetest music.

Saturday, November 7

I am writing this letter on the night train from Baltimore to Washington. Earlier this evening my family and I attended Bridget and James's wedding. The ceremony took place at a Roman Catholic cathedral that was bedecked with flowers and filled with music that must have been composed in heaven.

The guests that crowded the pews were strikingly dramatic. There were guests from the world of Drama: actresses in jewel-colored gowns, actors in sable cloaks, and musicians, dancers, and composers.

There were guests from the Peabody Conservatory of

Music: bearded professors with ribboned monocles in one eye and scrub-faced students who are studying Voice under James's tutelage. And there were guests from the War hospitals: doctors in dark suits, nurses in modest gowns, and former patients dressed in civilian clothes who bore the Marks of War—a missing eye or leg or arm. I soon discovered that the Veterans were amongst the wounded that James had helped heal through his music. During the ceremony those honorable men kept their eyes on the altar where James stood, his bride's tiny hand resting on his arm just above the brass hook at its end.

Mrs. Kilmar sat in the front pew. Her face was radiant as she gazed upon the faces of her beloved son and her new daughter. Later, during the reception, she confided happy news to my mother. Even though James now instructs Voice classes at Peabody, he travels much of the year to other cities to perform. Bridget plans to accompany her husband and so they have asked Mrs. Kilmar to reside with them. She will be pleasant company when the newlyweds are home, and when they are away she will keep careful watch over their household.

Regina, as I sit here on the train my thoughts return to that train ride I took as a child. In my mind's eye I see once more the fevered, blanket-wrapped boy-soldier bravely telling me of his part in the Struggle for our Nation's Reunification. I hear again the excitement in his boyish voice as he confided his love of music. I remember, too, how ill I became when I discovered that James had sacrificed both hands. My thoughts hurry forward to that day when I first heard his rich voice floating up through the pipes of the Post Office, and I smile at the sweet memory of James's reunion with his mother on that long-ago Christmas Eve. So much time has passed since I first met him, but I look forward to the years of friendship ahead.

P.S.—Attending weddings reminds me that I still have complete possession of my heart. At times I think about Boudy and recall the love of my Poet, John, but other gentlemen interest me little. Is it possible that sculpting has dulled my heart? Earlier tonight, when I watched Bridget and James's carriage drive away, I vowed to myself that once my statue is finished I will make my heart available.

Friday, November 13

Boudy has written me a letter. A brief letter of few words. Words that have numbed my heart. He wrote that he will wed in the new year.

Boudy wrote that he met his betrothed in court when he served as legal counsel for her brother. That is all I know of her, for he didn't mention her name, or describe her in any way, or add that he loved her. And then he closed his letter as he once did, with a declaration that his love for me is eternal.

How confused I am. If Boudy still loves me, why would he marry another? And yet, why not, for I have rejected his proposals. Do I love him? Yes, oh yes, Regina! Do I want to marry him? No, for I cannot tolerate the anger that has changed him into a stranger my heart refuses to recognize.

How I dread the approach of night, for the darkness reminds me that I am alone.

Thursday, Christmas Eve

This holiday season will be especially memorable for you and Michael with two children sleeping in their cradles. I grow impatient to meet your husband and to hold your little son and daughter in my arms. My statue is nearly completed—soon I will have the freedom to visit you, my dear, dear friend.

This morning I decided to work for a while on the sculpture (I am draping a cloak over Mr. Lincoln's suit). On arrival at the Capitol I became alarmed, for the building was frigid. I ran downstairs to my studio, and as I had feared, my birds were lying half-frozen on the floors of their cages. I snatched the cages off their hooks and rushed over to the stove to stoke up the fire. One bird had died, but the sudden warmth soon revived the other canaries. All the while I looked about the room, hoping to spy my dove, Poet, but he was nowhere to be seen. My search became frantic, and at last I found him trembling under a pile of rags. Before leaving the building I pleaded with the guards to watch over the fire in my stove so that it would burn throughout the night.

My parents are faring well, in health and spirit. Ma misses my brother dearly, but at least he writes to her faithfully. Of late, Pa has been so healthy that we believe he may pass this winter without suffering from his rheumatism.

We spent Christmas Eve at Mary's home. Her husband is merry the whole year through, but during the holiday season he becomes as excited as his young daughters. Before our arrival he had placed fir trees throughout the house, strung garlands of holly across every door, and hung the stockings on the mantel. Supper was a feast of delicate meats and golden pastries, and afterwards Mary and her little daughters presented a clever rendition of Mr. Dickens' story A Christmas Carol (my sister wore a paper beard and played the part of Scrooge).

I must close now, for we are preparing to go to Church. I may not be able to sing tonight, for my throat feels raw and sore in spite of the honeyed tea I have drunk all day. Merry Christmas, Regina, to you and your husband and children. May the New Year bring blessings to us all.

1869

1 8 6 9

My dear friend Regina,

My family's hope that Pa would escape an attack of rheumatism this winter has been dashed. For several days my beloved father was desperately ill. The day before yesterday his legs were so swollen that he couldn't walk without agonizing pain. Ma begged him to stay home from work, and he agreed, but he has now returned to his office. He had great worries that in his absence a younger, healthier man would be given his position.

With nothing I could do for Pa at home, I spent many long hours at my studio. The statue is near completion—only the shoes remain.

Oh, Regina, I fervently hope that the government approves my statue and I am given the money I have labored to earn! My parents are still unaware of my plan to take them with me to Rome—surely under the warm Mediterranean sun or in the healing waters Pa could recover his health. (I have heard of mineral springs in Italy where people bathe for miraculous cures.)

I shall close now, for I must rest—tomorrow I shall work from dawn to dusk on the final shaping of plaster into shoes. I still remember how Mr. Lincoln's giant feet ached so horribly that he often wore felt slippers in his office. The shoes that I am giving his statue must be comfortable above all else!

Saturday, January 30

The statue is completed! This afternoon I received the Interior Secretary, Mr. O. H. Browning, at my studio. Mr. Browning was a close acquaintance of Mr. Lincoln for more than thirty years.

He approved of my statue, Regina! He approved wholeheartedly! I noted the satisfaction on his face even before he spoke. He walked around and around the statue, looking all the while as if he were facing an old friend. Tears wetted his eyes, and when he spoke at last, he said, "Your statue bears a faithful resemblance to the original." Flattered by his generous words, I took his gloved hand and curtsied low. At that very moment the anxiety that had long plagued my heart flitted away. I looked at my parents (they had accompanied me, for they shared my concern that the statue might not please Mr. Browning). Ma and Pa were smiling widely, and I realized then that I too was smiling.

Mr. Browning left soon after with a promise to recommend that Congress make the first payment of $5,000. Even as the door closed behind him, I sat my parents down by the stove and poured out cups of tea. Ma was so excited that she didn't realize she had added five lumps of sugar to her cup. Pa kept looking from me to the statue, as though he expected one or the other to vanish from his sight like a sleeper's fading dream.

Regina, all at once I couldn't hide my secret from them a moment longer—I told my parents of my plan to take them with me to Italy. I told Ma about the shops and gardens and museums we could visit, and she sat there stunned into silence. I told Pa about Italy's warm mineral springs that could heal his swollen legs, but he shook his head no and told me that he must work for his living. Oh, Regina, I couldn't bear the thought of leaving Pa behind! I threw myself from my chair and flung my arms around him—I begged him to retire—I reminded him of my sudden wealth that could support us all—and Pa, too, fell into a stunned silence.

On our walk home my parents' silence disappeared at last, for they had a thousand and one things to say in their excite-

ment. They are both downstairs in the kitchen preparing a celebratory supper, and I am upstairs at my desk, thinking, as I
sometimes do, about the years that have passed by. I first sat at
this desk when I was a girl of thirteen to write a letter to you,
Regina, and now at twenty-one years I can think of no one else
to whom I would rather write in my happiness. Soon, dear
friend, we will meet again. For now, though, I must close this
letter, for I have spotted Perry's carriage at our door and already
Mary and her daughters are tumbling out.

Monday, March 15

Thank you, Regina, for sending me the reviews from your New
York newspapers. I have been mailed other articles about my
statue from newspapers across our Union. Happily, each review
pleases me—not only because my work is judged successful
(which I confess gives me much satisfaction), but also because
of what the warm response reveals about the people of our
Nation—that we remain devoted to our Martyr President.

Since you so kindly asked, Regina, I am only too glad to
describe my statue to you. As you know, the statue is life-size
and exactly proportioned to the man himself. The sculpted Mr.
Lincoln stands tall but in a natural pose, just as the actual man
often stood at the window in his office.

The face is modeled truthfully without softening the features that some thought ugly—in my view, his actual face was
beautified by his expression of gentle compassion. I took great
care in sculpting the locks of hair to reveal its coarseness and
thickness and to give the impression that Mr. Lincoln had just
pushed his fingers through his hair—just as the actual man so
often did. The head is bent forward slightly, as though Mr. Lincoln is reading the papyrus scroll held in his right hand. On the

scroll I carved out words that refer to the Emancipation Proclamation (surely the abolition of slavery was one of Mr. Lincoln's
greatest acts).

I gave Mr. Lincoln a circular cloak—it sweeps over his right
shoulder and arm, drops backwards off his left shoulder, and is
tucked up under the forearm and held up by his left hand. The
cloak has purpose, for it symbolizes Mr. Lincoln's promise that
the Government will cloak, as if in a protective mantle, those
who have been freed. The cloak also adds dignity, for I wanted
to dispel the myth that the actual Mr. Lincoln had the appearance of a backwoodsman. The hem rests on the ground, afford-
ing me a way to support the statue's great weight.

Now I look forward to the pleasant chore of finding a block
of the purest, whitest marble that Italy can offer!

Since February, the statue has been on display in my studio to the members of Congress. Soon—quite soon, in fact—
a packing company will box it up and deliver it to the seaport
in New York City. My parents and I will accompany the statue
to New York—I want to be certain that it arrives safely and is
sheltered properly until our ship sails in June. As soon as I
arrange storage for the statue, my parents and I will hire a carriage to drive us to your home. We should arrive on the evening
of April fifth. I look forward to our happy reunion, dear friend.

But there is much to do before our departure. Whenever I
can escape from the chores of ironing our clothes and packing
our trunks, I call on old friends to bid them adieu. Imagine,
Regina, I shall not walk down the streets of my beloved Washington for two long years, but I shall enjoy exploring the streets
of Rome.

One friend I will miss dreadfully is Senator Ross. By the
time of our return he will have reached the end of his senato-

rial term and will, because of his role in the Impeachment, be forced to retire from political life. Ever since the trial Senator Ross has been worried about the safety of his family in Kansas. Indeed, his wife and children have been physically attacked and threatened with death. He never did find a suitable house for them in Washington, but Pa has invited the family to lodge in our home during our absence. Ma, delighted by the arrangement, is scouring the entire house inch by inch before Mrs. Ross's arrival.

Last month Pa finally retired from the War Department (he was given a handsome gold watch on a long chain). He spends most of his hours visiting with Mary's daughters. Surely they will miss their grandfather dearly, for he spoils all five.

I have nearly completed my shopping. What fun Ma and I have had buying shoes and gowns and hats and capes for ourselves and suits of fine cloth for Pa! Yesterday I purchased a traveling cage for my dove, Poet, for he will accompany me to Rome (I have given my canaries to Mary's little girls).

Until we see each other in April, dear friend, stay well.

Monday, June 7

This morning, as Ma, Pa, and I drove away from your home, sunlight flooded the carriage and revealed the fatigue aging my parents' faces. I thought to myself that it is sheer madness to rush my mother and father across Europe to Italy—sheer and utter madness! I decided at once that they must find quietude and pleasure on this trip, for none deserve a holiday more.

This, then, is my new plan. When our ship docks in Le Havre, France, I will hire an agent to escort the statue to the studio I've leased in Rome. Then I shall take Ma and Pa on a leisurely journey across the Continent. My search for the perfect block of marble must wait a few months.

How can I ever thank you and Michael for your gracious hospitality? Our wonderful visit, though two months long, was still too brief, for we would need years to speak of all the things our letters never mentioned.

And thank you for your beautiful gift. I have named the little dove after you, Regina, and so whenever I look upon my cage I will be reminded of my most cherished friends, you and my Poet, John.

How blessed you are, Regina. Johnny and Nellie are tiny angels! (Ma still marvels that neither baby cried at the Christening despite their teething.) And your husband's devotion to you and the children endears him to me.

Regina, your heart must be a crowded place—surely it is overfilled with love for Michael and the twins. I have long denied my heart such joy, for my work on the statue demanded all of me. Oh, Regina, at times I liken myself to a block of marble, waiting for Love to sculpt me into someone of fervent heart.

I must close quickly and post this letter before we board the ship. Until I write again, Regina, remember me with fondness as your dearest friend, Vinnie.

EPILOGUE

Vinnie stayed in Rome for two years, sculpting. Upon her return to Washington, her marble statue of Lincoln was declared a great success; it still stands in the Rotunda of the Capitol building. After her marriage in 1878 to Lieutenant Richard Hoxie, she gave up sculpting to devote herself to her husband and later to their son, Richie. Eventually Vinnie returned to her art. She also enjoyed performing on the harp and working with blind children. After a long struggle with a kidney ailment, Vinnie Ream died in Washington on November 14, 1914, and was buried in Arlington National Cemetery.

LETTER FROM THE AUTHOR

Dear Reader,

All my life I have admired those who courageously pursue their dreams with hands, heart, and soul. Vinnie Ream was such a dreamer. Indeed, despite her tiny size, she must have possessed the courage of a giant to achieve her dream of sculpting.

I was an adult before I came across Vinnie's name and a brief description of her achievements. Immediately intrigued and yet puzzled that I had not heard of her earlier, I asked others about her; no one I asked had heard of her either. For the next nine months I researched Vinnie's life, the Civil War, and the art of sculpting, and then one day I forced myself to close the books and pick up my pen. As I sat at my desk I wondered how Vinnie would have told her story. The answer was obvious: through correspondence with a trusted friend.

I had read hundreds of letters written during the Civil War era and had noted traits common to all of them. Whether their writers were rich or poor, educated or not, young or old, male or female, the letters were written in a formal tone, with a wonderfully expressive vocabulary. All the letters conveyed emotion; there seemed to be no hesitancy to write about fear or sorrow or joy. There were stylistic similarities as well, such as a liberal use of capitalization and dashes within sentences to emphasize important words or ideas. To keep the tone of this book as historically correct as possible, I tried to follow most of the stylistic practices of the time. However, in some instances where historical practice might have distracted the reader—for example, when lowercase letters were used in words that are now capitalized—I conformed with modern usage.

Although few of Vinnie's personal letters have been found, I found her voice by studying her poetry and journals and by reading a few quotations in newspaper articles. For example, in speaking to a reporter about her sessions sculpting President Lincoln, Vinnie said, "These visits to the White House continued for five months. Through all this time the personality of Lincoln was gradually sinking deeper and deeper into my soul. I was modeling the man in clay, but he was being engraven still more deeply upon my heart." Borrowing Vinnie's words, I created other references to her heart to express emotions, such as "I felt my heart lift like a kite in the wind" and "My heart is swollen with fear." Her plea that John write her a poem, her description of Lincoln's two faces of sorrow, her declaration of devastation upon hearing of his assassination, and her comparison of his coffin's sunlit nails to stars—all these are Vinnie's own.

Leaning on Gordon Langley Hall's *Vinnie Ream: The Story of the Girl Who Sculpted Lincoln*, Carl Sandburg's definitive books about Abraham Lincoln, Freeman H. Hubbard's *Vinnie Ream and Mr. Lincoln*, on the archives of the Library of Congress, I wrote letters from Vinnie to Regina, a friend I imagined for her. As I took Vinnie on her remarkable journey from Fort Smith, Arkansas, to the docks of New York City, I mentioned actual historical figures of military, political, and artistic importance, among them Civil War generals, Frederick Douglass, senators and representatives, journalists, sculptors, and actors who performed in Washington in the 1860s. There was no need to fictionalize their roles in history or their presence in Vinnie's life—for example, Senator Edmund Ross of Kansas was a boarder in the Reams' home, Ulysses S. Grant did compliment Vinnie's singing, and her studio was actually used for secret meetings during the impeachment trial of President Johnson. I presented the members of Vinnie's family and the Cherokee cousins John Rollin Ridge and Elias Cornelius Boudinot as truthfully as possible, adding fictional details to shape them into rounded characters. Two fictional characters, both soldiers, were created to cast light into less well illuminated corners of Vinnie's life—James Kilmar was introduced to reveal Vinnie's documented gifts as a musician and singer, and Nathan Ennis was invented as a way to explore the depth of Vinnie's sorrow about the Civil War.

All the major events of Vinnie's life happened as written, but I used my imagination to add details where none are known. For example, I knew that wounds were dangerous in that era; if a cut became infected and gangrene developed, the usual consequence was amputation. I reasoned that at some point Vinnie would have cut herself on a sculpting tool, so I had to heal her. But how? I remembered hearing years ago, when I lived in the west of Ireland, that in the centuries before antibiotics the villagers placed bread in the darkest corners of their cottages so that mold would grow on it. Whenever someone suffered an infection or fever, the mold was eaten. I loaned the Irish custom to Vinnie's Scottish mother, and the letter about the mold cure came about.

Vinnie's personality needed no fictionalizing. From all the evidence, Vinnie was a compassionate person, a devoted daughter, a fierce patriot, and a joyous lover of music and poetry. Above all, she was a dreamer—a courageous dreamer.

Yours truly,

Maureen Stack Sappéy